NEW YORK

S0-AZS-475

THE KINGFISHER BOOK OF

Great
GIRL
Stories

KINGFISHER
Larousse Kingfisher Chambers Inc.
80 Maiden Lane
New York, New York 10038
www.kingfisherpub.com

First published in 1999
2 4 6 8 10 9 7 5 3 1
1SBC/1201/SC/RNB/157MA

This selection, introductions, and foreword
copyright © Rosemary Sandberg 1999
Cover painting *Under the Spreading Chestnut Tree*
by Albert Thomas Jarvis Gilbert, courtesy of
Mark Hancock, Fine Art Photographic Library Ltd.
Text and illustrations copyright © individual
authors and artists; see Acknowledgments.

The acknowledgments on page 160 constitute
an extension of this copyright page.

All rights reserved under International and
Pan-American Copyright Conventions

LIBRARY OF CONGRESS CATALOGING-IN-PUBLICATION DATA
has been applied for.

ISBN 0-7534-5551-X

Designed by Ian Butterworth
Printed in Hong Kong

THE KINGFISHER BOOK OF
Great GIRL Stories

A TREASURY OF CLASSICS FROM CHILDREN'S LITERATURE

Chosen by Rosemary Sandberg

CONTENTS

FOREWORD

When I was young, I used to hide away with a favorite book and pretend 1 was someone else. The first person I wanted to be was Milly-Molly-Mandy. I could imagine living in a nice white cottage and playing with little-friend-Susan and Billy Blunt, with my dog Toby always at my side. When I was seven, I joined the library. I was immensely proud to have *my own card* and started to work my way through the shelves. My choice would reflect my mood. Longing for company, I found a friend in Katy Carr and shared her dreams of freedom. Feeling momentarily despondent, I turned my back on my own life and slipped into that of Anne of Green Gables, an orphan whose resilience and outspokenness often led to trouble. How I envied her pluck, and wanted it for my own! Then, ready for excitement, I was drawn to Dorothy and her fabulous adventures along the Yellow Brick Road in the Land of Oz.

I realize that many of the characters I especially enjoyed were girls. I also read books about boys—plenty of them! But I felt a special closeness to the girl characters, recognizing myself in them, taking comfort from discovering that other girls could be unhappy and misunderstood, or bold and rebellious. Later, I watched history repeat itself with my two daughters, both avid readers. One, like me, loved reading about Milly-Molly-Mandy. The other much preferred Pippi Longstocking, and longed to live all alone just like her, wearing whatever she wanted, and behaving any way she pleased. When I was a children's book publisher, I discovered new girl characters with whom I identified, even though I was long grown up. I was always pleased to be able to introduce strong female characters to new readers, hoping they would identify with them as I had, and be enthralled by their resourcefulness, courage, and sense of adventure.

In this collection I have gathered together interesting, spirited girls who have a zest for life, and who grow in the imagination so that they become as close as good friends. Several of the stories were written many years ago, but their popularity is timeless. Each generation delights in their discovery. Others are much more recent, but they, too, touch the reader in a way that earns them the status of contemporary classics. Why is a book recommended by one generation to the next? I think it is the author's ability to create living characters whom we recognize. It is the indefinable mix of the familiar and the unexpected in a character's behavior that singles out the great books and gives them a permanent place in our hearts.

So please dip into a wonderful mix of stories that will delight and intrigue you. I have written a short introduction to each one that I hope will encourage you to seek out the books from which they come—there are many more adventures to enjoy. Maybe someone will read these stories aloud to you. Or maybe, like me, you will hide away by yourself, meeting new friends in the stories—and perhaps even pretending, for a little while, to be someone else.

Rosemary Sandberg
June 1999

Introduction

Milly-Molly-Mandy lives with Father, Mother, Grandma and Grandpa, Aunty, Uncle, and Toby the dog in a little white house with a thatched roof. She has short hair and short legs, but a very long name: Millicent Margaret Amanda, or Milly-Molly-Mandy for short and for everyday. She has all sorts of adventures with little-friend-Susan and Billy Blunt, and sometimes she likes playing on her own. One day she decides to give a party, so, with the help of her friends, she starts to plan. And somehow the guest list gets longer and longer . . . .

MILLY ~ MOLLY ~ MANDY

JOYCE LANKESTER BRISLEY

Milly~Molly~Mandy Gives a Party

Once upon a time Milly-Molly-Mandy had a plan. And when she had thought over the plan for a while she went to look in her moneybox. And in the moneybox were four pennies and a ha'penny, which Milly-Molly-Mandy did not think would be enough for her plan. So Milly-Molly-Mandy went off to talk it over with her little-friend-Susan down the road.

"Susan," said Milly-Molly-Mandy, "I've got a plan (only it's a great secret). I want to give a party in our barn to Farver and Muvver and Grandpa and Grandma and Uncle and Aunty. And I want to buy refreshments. And you and I will be waitresses. And if there's anything over we can eat it up afterwards."

Little-friend-Susan thought it a very good plan indeed.

"Will we wear caps?" she asked.

"Yes," said Milly-Molly-Mandy, "and aprons. Only I haven't got enough money for the refreshments, so I don't think there'll be any over. We must think."

So Milly-Molly-Mandy and little-friend-Susan sat down and thought hard.

"We must work and earn some," said Milly-Molly-Mandy.

"But how?" said little-friend-Susan.

"We might sell something," said Milly-Molly-Mandy.

"But what?" said little-friend-Susan.

So they had to think some more.

Presently Milly-Molly-Mandy said, "I've got pansies and marigolds in my garden."

And little-friend-Susan said, "I've got nasturtiums in mine."

"We could run errands for people," said Milly-Molly-Mandy.

"And clean brass," said little-friend-Susan.

That was a lovely idea, so Milly-Molly-Mandy fetched a pencil and paper and wrote out very carefully:

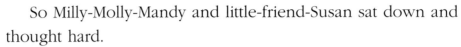
Millicent Margaret Amanda & Susan & Co. have bunches of flowers for sale and clean brass very cheap (we do not spill the polish) and run errands very cheap.

"What's 'and Co.'?" said little-friend-Susan.

"It's just business," said Milly-Molly-Mandy, "but perhaps we might ask Billy Blunt to be it. And he could be a waiter."

Then they hung the notice on the front gate, and waited just the other side of the hedge.

Several people passed, but nobody seemed to want anything. Then at last a motorcar came along with a lady and gentleman in it; and when they saw the nice white cottage with the thatched roof they stopped at the gate to ask if they could get some cream there.

Milly-Molly-Mandy said, "I'll go and ask Muvver," and took the little pot they held out. And when she came back with it full of cream the lady and gentleman had read the notice and were asking little-friend-Susan questions. As the lady paid for the cream she said they must certainly have some flowers. So they each bought a bunch. And then the gentleman said the round brass thing in front of his car needed cleaning very badly—could the firm do it straight away?

So Milly-Molly-Mandy said, "Yes, sir," and raced back to the cottage to give Mother the cream money and to borrow the brass polishing box. And then she cleaned the round brass thing in front of the car with one piece of cloth and little-friend-Susan rubbed it bright with another piece of cloth, and the lady and gentleman looked on and seemed very satisfied.

Then the gentleman asked, "How much?" and paid them two pence for the flowers and a penny for the polishing. Milly-Molly-Mandy wanted to do some more polishing for the money, but the gentleman said they couldn't stop. And then they said good-bye and went off, and the lady turned and waved, and Milly-Molly-Mandy and little-friend-Susan waved back until they were gone.

Milly-Molly-Mandy and little-friend-Susan felt very happy and pleased.

And now they had sevenpence ha'penny for the refreshments. Father and Mother and Grandpa and Grandma and Uncle and

Aunty and Mrs. Moggs, little-friend-Susan's mother, made seven.

Then who should look over the hedge but Mr. Jakes, the Postman, on his way home from collecting letters from the letterboxes. He had seen the notice on the gate.

"What's this? You trying to make a fortune?" said the Postman.

"Yes," said Milly-Molly-Mandy, "we've earned threepence!"

"My! And what do you plan to do with it?" said the Postman.

"We've got a secret!" said Milly-Molly-Mandy, with a little skip.

"Ah!" said the Postman. "I guess it's a nice one, too!"

Milly-Molly-Mandy looked at little-friend-Susan, and then she looked at the Postman. He was a nice Postman. "You won't tell if we tell you?" she asked.

"Try me!" said the Postman promptly. So Milly-Molly-Mandy told him they were planning to give a party to Father and Mother and Grandpa and Grandma and Uncle and Aunty and Mrs. Moggs.

"They're in luck, they are!" said the Postman. "Nobody asks me to parties."

Milly-Molly-Mandy looked at little-friend-Susan again, and then she looked at the Postman. He was a very nice Postman. Then she said, "Supposing you were invited, would you come?"

"You try me!" said the Postman promptly again. And then he hitched up his letterbag and went on.

"Farver and Muvver and Grandpa and Grandma and Uncle and Aunty and Mrs. Moggs and the Postman. We've got to earn some more," said Milly-Molly-Mandy. "Let's go down to the village and ask Billy Blunt to be 'and Co.', and p'r'aps he'll have an idea."

Billy Blunt was in the road outside the cornshop, mending the handles of his box on wheels. He had made it nearly all himself, and it was a very nice one, painted green like the waterbutt and the lawn roller. He thought "and Co." was rather a funny name, but he said he would be it all right, and offered to make them a box with a slit in it, where they could keep their earnings. And he put in four farthings out of his collection. (Billy Blunt was collecting farthings—he had nineteen in an empty birdseed bag.)

So now they had eightpence ha'penny for the refreshments.

On Monday morning, on their way home to dinner, Milly-Molly-Mandy and little-friend-Susan passed Mrs. Jakes, the Postman's wife, at her door, getting a breath of fresh air before dishing up her dinner. And Mrs. Jakes said, "Good morning! How's the firm of Millicent Margaret Amanda, Susan, and Co. getting on?"

Milly-Molly-Mandy said, "Very well, thank you!"

"My husband's told me about your brass cleaning," said Mrs. Jakes. "I've got a whole mantelshelf-full that wants doing!"

Milly-Molly-Mandy and little-friend-Susan were very pleased, and arranged to come in directly after school was over in the afternoon and clean it.

And they cleaned a mug and three candlesticks and two lamps—one big and one little—and a tray and a warming pan, and they didn't spill or waste any of the polish. Mrs. Jakes seemed very satisfied, and gave them each a penny and a piece of cake.

So now they had tenpence ha'penny for refreshments.

But when they got outside Milly-Molly-Mandy said, "Farver and Muvver and Grandpa and Grandma and Uncle and Aunty and Mrs. Moggs and the Postman and Mrs. Postman—I wonder if we've earned enough, Susan?"

As they turned home they passed the forge, and of course they had to stop a moment at the doorway, as usual, to watch the fire roaring, and Mr. Rudge the Blacksmith banging with his hammer on the anvil.

Little-friend-Susan was just a bit nervous of the Blacksmith—he was so big, and his face was so dirty it made his teeth look very white and his eyes very twinkly when he smiled at them. But Milly-Molly-Mandy knew he was nice and clean under the dirt, which he couldn't help while he worked. So she smiled back.

And the Blacksmith said, "Hello!"

And Milly-Molly-Mandy said, "Hello!"

Then the Blacksmith beckoned with his finger and said, "Come here!"

Milly-Molly-Mandy gave a little jump, and little-friend-Susan pulled at her hand, but Milly-Molly-Mandy knew he was really just a nice man under the dirt, so she went up to him.

And the Blacksmith said, "Look what I've got here!" And he showed them a tiny little horseshoe, just like a proper one, only smaller, which he had made for them to keep. Milly-Molly-Mandy and little-friend-Susan were pleased!

Milly-Molly-Mandy thanked him very much. And then she looked at the Blacksmith and said, "If you were invited to a party, would you come?"

And the Blacksmith looked at Milly-Molly-Mandy with twinkly eyes and said he'd come quite fast—so long as it wasn't before five o'clock on Saturday, when he was playing cricket with his team in the meadow.

When they got outside again Milly-Molly-Mandy said, "Farver and Muvver and Grandpa and Grandma and Uncle and Aunty and Mrs. Moggs and the Postman and Mrs. Postman and the Blacksmith. We'll ask them for half past five, and we ought to earn some more money, Susan!"

Just then they met Billy Blunt coming along, pulling his box on wheels with a bundle in it. And Billy Blunt grinned and said,

"I'm fetching Mrs. Bloss's wash¡ , for the firm!" Milly-Molly-Mandy and little-friend-Susan were pl ⌒ed!

When Saturday morning c ne, all the invitations had been given out, and the firm of M licent Margaret Amanda, Susan, and Co. was very busy putting things tidy in the barn, and covering up things that couldn't be moved with lots of green branches, which Grandpa was trimming from the hedges.

And when half past five came Milly-Molly-Mandy and little-friend-Susan, with clean hands and paper caps and aprons, waited by the barn door to welcome the guests. And each gentleman received a marigold buttonhole, and each lady a pansy.

Everybody arrived in good time, except the Blacksmith, who was just a little bit late—he looked so clean and pink in his white cricket flannels, Milly-Molly-Mandy hardly knew him—and Billy Blunt. But Billy Blunt came lugging a gramophone and two records which he had borrowed from a bigger boy at school. (He never told, but he had given the boy all the rest of his collection of farthings—fifteen of them, which makes threepence three farthings—in exchange.)

Then Billy Blunt, who didn't want to dance, looked after the gramophone, while Father and Mother and Grandpa and Grandma and Uncle and Aunty and Mrs. Moggs and the Postman and Mrs. Postman and the Blacksmith and Milly-Molly-Mandy and little-friend-Susan danced together in the old barn till the dust flew. And Milly-Molly-Mandy danced a lot with the Blacksmith as well as with everybody else, and so did little-friend-Susan.

They did enjoy themselves!

And then there were refreshments—raspberry drops and aniseed balls on saucers trimmed with little flowers; and late

blackberries on leaf plates; and s̶ ̶bet drinks, which Billy Blunt prepared while Milly-Molly-Mand̶ ̶ ̶d little-friend-Susan stood by to tell people just the very moment ̶ ̶ drink, when it was fizzing properly. (It was exciting!) And a jelly which Milly-Molly-Mandy and little-friend-Susan had made themselves from a packet, only it had to be eaten rather like soup, as it wouldn't stand up properly.

But Father and Mother and Grandpa and Grandma and Uncle and Aunty and Mrs. Moggs and the Postman and Mrs. Postman and the Blacksmith all said they had never enjoyed a jelly so much.

And the Blacksmith, in a big voice, proposed a vote of thanks to the firm for the delightful party and refreshments, and everybody else said "Hear! Hear!" and clapped. And Milly-Molly-Mandy and little-friend-Susan joined in the clapping too, which wasn't quite proper, but they were so happy they couldn't help it!

And then all the guests went home.

And when the firm came to clear up the refreshments they found there was only one aniseed ball left. But placed among the empty saucers and glasses on the bench were a small basket of pears and a bag of mixed sweets with a ticket "For the Waiter and Waitresses" on it!

Introduction

Ramona Quimby never thinks of herself as a pest, but her overenthusiastic antics always seem to land her in trouble. When you are the youngest in the family and the youngest person on your street, you have to make a great big noisy fuss just to get noticed. But now that she is going to school, Ramona tries hard to be good. At rest time she wants to be the wake-up fairy, so she gives a little snore to show what a good rester she is—but when the other children start to snore and giggle, her friend Howie says, "Ramona started it!" That isn't her fault, is it? When Halloween comes around, everyone dresses up for the school parade. Howie wants to be a pirate, but ends up having to wear his sister's old cat costume—with a broken tail. Ramona decides to be the baddest witch in the parade, in a scary, flabby mask. Now she can be as naughty as she likes.

RAMONA THE PEST

BEVERLY CLEARY

The Baddest Witch in the World

When they were in sight of the playground, Ramona saw that it was already swarming with both the morning and the afternoon kindergartens in their Halloween costumes. Poor Miss Binny, dressed like Mother Goose, now had the responsibility of sixty-eight boys and girls. "Run along, Ramona," said Mrs. Quimby, when they had crossed the street. "Howie's mother and I will go around to the big playground and try to find a seat on a bench before they are all taken."

Ramona ran screaming onto the playground. "Yah! Yah! I'm the baddest witch in the world!" Nobody paid any attention, because everyone else was screaming, too. The noise was glorious. Ramona yelled and screamed and shrieked and chased anyone who would run. She chased tramps and ghosts and ballerinas. Sometimes other witches in masks exactly like hers chased her, and then she would

turn around and chase the witches right back. She tried to chase Howie, but he would not run. He just stood beside the fence holding his broken tail and missing all the fun.

Ramona discovered dear little Davy in a skimpy pirate costume from the toy store. She could tell he was Davy by his thin legs. At last! She pounced and kissed him through her rubber mask. Davy looked startled, but he had the presence of mind to make a gagging noise while Ramona raced away, satisfied that she finally had managed to catch and kiss Davy.

Then Ramona saw Susan getting out of her mother's car. As she might have guessed, Susan was dressed as an old-fashioned girl with a long skirt, an apron, and pantalettes. "I'm the baddest witch in the world!" yelled Ramona, and ran after Susan, whose curls bobbed daintily about her shoulders in a way that could not be disguised. Ramona was unable to resist. After weeks of longing she tweaked one of Susan's curls, and yelled "*Boing!*" through her rubber mask.

"You stop that," said Susan, and smoothed her curls.

"Yah! Yah! I'm the baddest witch in the world!" Ramona was carried away. She tweaked another curl and yelled another muffled "*Boing!*"

A clown laughed and joined Ramona. He too tweaked a curl and yelled, "*Boing!*"

The old-fashioned girl stamped her foot. "You stop that!" she said angrily.

"*Boing! Boing!*" Others joined the game. Susan tried to run away, but no matter which way she ran there was someone eager to stretch a curl and yell, "*Boing!*" Susan ran to Miss Binny. "Miss Binny! Miss Binny!" she cried. "They're teasing me! They're pulling my hair and boinging me!"

"Who's teasing you?" asked Miss Binny.

"Everybody," said Susan tearfully. "A witch started it."

"Which witch?" asked Miss Binny.

Susan looked around. "I don't know which witch," she said, "but it was a bad witch."

That's me, the baddest witch in the world, thought Ramona. At the same time she was a little surprised. That others really would not know that she was behind her mask had never occurred to her.

"Never mind, Susan," said Miss Binny. "You stay near me, and no one will tease you."

Which witch, thought Ramona, liking the sound of the words. Which witch, which witch. As the words ran through her thoughts Ramona began to wonder if Miss Binny could guess who she was. She ran up to her teacher and shouted in her muffled voice, "Hello, Miss Binny! I'm going to get you, Miss Binny!"

"Ooh, what a scary witch!" said Miss Binny, rather absent-mindedly, Ramona thought. Plainly Miss Binny was not really

frightened, and with so many witches running around she had not recognized Ramona.

No, Miss Binny was not the one who was frightened. Ramona was. Miss Binny did not know who this witch was. Nobody knew who Ramona was, and if nobody knew who she was, she wasn't anybody.

"Get out of the way, old witch!" Eric R. yelled at Ramona. He did not say, "Get out of the way, Ramona."

Ramona could not remember a time when there was not someone near who knew who she was. Even last Halloween, when she dressed up as a ghost and went trick-or-treating with Beezus and the older boys and girls, everyone seemed to know who she was. "I can guess who this little ghost is," the neighbors said, as they dropped a miniature candy bar or a handful of peanuts into her paper bag. And now, with so many witches running around and still more witches on the big playground, no one knew who she was.

"Davy, guess who I am!" yelled Ramona. Surely Davy would know.

"You're just another old witch," answered Davy.

The feeling was the scariest one Ramona had ever experienced. She felt lost inside her costume. She wondered if her mother would know which witch was which, and the thought that her own mother might not know her frightened Ramona even more. What if her mother forgot her? What if everyone in the whole world forgot her? With that terrifying thought, Ramona snatched off her mask, and although its ugliness was no longer the most frightening thing about it, she rolled it up so she would not have to look at it.

How cool the air felt outside that dreadful mask! Ramona no longer wanted to be the baddest witch in the world. She wanted to be Ramona Geraldine Quimby and be sure that Miss Binny and everyone on the playground knew her. Around her the ghosts and tramps and pirates raced and shouted, but Ramona stood near the door of the kindergarten quietly watching.

Davy raced up to her and yelled, "Yah! You can't catch me!"

"I don't want to catch you," Ramona informed him.

Davy looked surprised and a little disappointed, but he ran off on his thin little legs, shouting, "Yo-ho-ho and a bottle of rum!"

Joey yelled after him, "You're not really a pirate. You're just Mush Pot Davy!"

Miss Binny was trying to herd her sixty-eight charges into a double line. Two mothers who felt sorry for the teacher were helping round up the kindergarten to start the Halloween parade, but, as always, there were some children who would rather run around than do what they were supposed to do. For once Ramona was not one of them. On the big playground someone started to play a marching record through a loudspeaker. The Halloween parade that Ramona had looked forward to since she was in nursery school was about to begin.

"Come along, children," said Miss Binny. Seeing Ramona standing alone, she said, "Come on, Ramona."

It was a great relief to Ramona to hear Miss Binny speak her name, to hear her teacher say "Ramona" when she was looking at her. But as much as Ramona longed to prance along to the marching music with the rest of her class, she did not move to join them.

"Put on your mask, Ramona, and get in line," said Miss Binny, guiding a ghost and a gypsy into place.

Ramona wanted to obey her teacher, but at the same time she was afraid of losing herself behind that scary mask. The line of kindergarteners, all of them wearing masks except Howie with his

pipe-cleaner whiskers, was less straggly now, and everyone was eager to start the parade. If Ramona did not do something quickly she would be left behind, and she could not let such a thing happen, not when she had waited so many years to be in a Halloween parade.

Ramona took only a moment to decide what to do. She ran to her cupboard inside the kindergarten building and snatched a crayon from her box. Then she grabbed a piece of paper from the supply cupboard. Outside she could hear the many feet of the morning and afternoon kindergartens marching off to the big playground. There was no time for Ramona's best printing, but that was all right. This job was not seat work to be supervised by Miss Binny. As fast as she could Ramona printed her name, and then she could not resist adding with a flourish her last initial, complete with ears and whiskers.

Now the whole world would know who she was! She was Ramona Quimby, the only girl in the world with ears and whiskers on her last initial. Ramona pulled on her rubber mask, clapped her pointed hat on top of it, snapped the elastic under her chin and ran after her class as it marched on to the big playground. She did not care if she was last in line and had to march beside gloomy old Howie, still lugging his broken tail.

Around the playground marched the kindergarten followed by the first grade and all the other grades while mothers and little brothers and sisters watched. Ramona felt very grown-up remembering how last year she had been a little sister sitting on a bench watching for her big sister Beezus to march by and hoping for a leftover doughnut.

"Yah! Yah! I'm the baddest witch in the world!" Ramona chanted, as she held up her sign for all to see. Around the playground she marched toward her mother, who was waiting on the bench. Her mother saw her, pointed her out to Mrs. Kemp, and waved. Ramona beamed inside her stuffy mask. Her mother recognized her!

Poor little Willa Jean in her stroller could not read, so Ramona called out to her, "It's me, Willa Jean. I'm Ramona, the baddest witch in the world!"

Willa Jean in her rabbit mask understood. She laughed and slapped her hands on the tray of her stroller.

Ramona saw Henry's dog Ribsy trotting along, supervising the parade. "Yah! Ribsy! I'm going to get you, Ribsy!" she threatened, as she marched past.

Ribsy gave a short bark, and Ramona was sure that even Ribsy knew who she was as she marched off to collect her doughnut and apple juice.

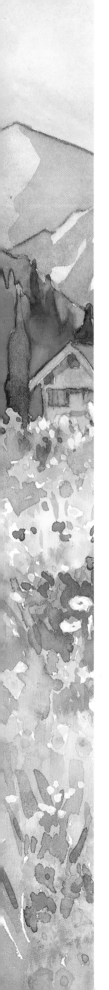

Introduction

Heidi is only five, and she has lived with her Aunt Detie since her mother died. But now that Detie has a job in far-off Frankfurt, the little girl goes to live with her grandfather in his cabin in the Swiss Alps. Up in the high pastures, Heidi meets young Peter, the goatherd. Like everyone in the small village of Dörfli, Peter knows Heidi's grandfather as "Uncle Alp." When Detie leaves her with the old man, it does not take Heidi long to settle into her new life. She delights in her freedom, running wild with the goats, climbing a ladder to sleep in the hayloft on a bed of fresh, sweet-smelling hay, and spending carefree days in the meadows with Peter and the goats.

HEIDI

JOHANNA SPYRI

A Day with the Goats

Heidi was awakened the next morning by a shrill whistle, and as she opened her eyes a beam of sunlight came through the hole in the wall, making the hay shine like gold. At first she could not think where she was, then she heard her grandfather's deep voice outside and remembered joyfully that she had come to live in the mountains. Now she jumped out of bed, full of excitement at all the new experiences awaiting her. She dressed herself as quickly as possible, then climbed down the ladder and hurried outside. Peter was waiting there with his herd, and her grandfather was just bringing Daisy and Dusky from their stall. She went to say good morning to them all.

"Do you want to go up to the pasture with Peter?" asked the old man. This idea clearly delighted her. "You must have a wash first, or the sun will laugh to see you so dirty."

He pointed to a tub full of water, standing in the sun beside the door, and Heidi went over to it at once and began to splash about. Uncle Alp went indoors, calling to Peter, "Come here, General of the goats, and bring your knapsack with you." Peter held out the

little bag that contained his meager lunch, and watched with big eyes as the old man put in a piece of bread and a piece of cheese, both twice as big as his own.

"Take this mug, too, and fill it for her twice at dinnertime. She doesn't know how to drink straight from the goat as you do. She'll stay with you all day, and mind you look after her and see that she doesn't fall down the ravine."

Heidi came running in. "The sun can't laugh at me now," she said. Her grandfather smilingly agreed. In her desire to please the sun, she had rubbed her face with the hard towel until she looked like a boiled lobster.

"When you come home tonight, you'll have to go right inside the tub like a fish, for you'll get black feet running about with the goats. Now off you go."

It was very beautiful on the mountain that morning. The night wind had blown all the clouds away and the sky was deep blue. The sun shone brilliantly on the green pasture and on the flowers, which were blooming everywhere. There were primroses, blue gentians, and dainty yellow rockroses. Heidi rushed to and fro, wild with excitement at the sight of them. She quite forgot Peter and the goats, and kept stopping to gather flowers and put them in her apron. She wanted to take them home to stick among the hay in her bedroom, to make it look like a meadow.

Peter needed eyes all around his head. It was more than one pair could do to watch Heidi as well as the goats, for they too were running about in all directions. He had to whistle and shout and swing his stick in the air to bring the wandering animals together.

"Where have you got to now, Heidi?" he called once, rather crossly.

"Here," came her voice from behind a little hillock some distance back. It was covered with primroses, which had a most delicious scent. Heidi had never smelled anything so lovely before and had sat down among them to enjoy it to the full.

"Come on," called Peter. "Uncle said I wasn't to let you fall over the ravine."

"Where's that?" she called, without moving.

"Right up above. We still have a long way to go, so do come on. Hear the old hawk croaking away up there?"

Heidi jumped up at this last remark and ran to him with her apron full of flowers.

"You've got enough now," he said, as they started to climb again. "Don't pick any more, otherwise you'll always be lagging behind, and besides, if you keep on, there won't be any left for tomorrow."

Heidi saw the sense of this, and anyway her apron was almost full. She kept close to Peter after that, and the goats went on in a more orderly fashion too, for now they could smell the fragrant herbs that grew on their grazing ground, which they loved and were anxious to reach.

Peter usually took up his quarters for the day at the very foot of a rocky mountain peak. On the steep slopes above, there were only a few bushes and stunted fir trees, and the summit itself was just bare rock. On one side was the sheer drop over the ravine that Uncle Alp had spoken of. When they reached this place, Peter took off his knapsack and laid it in a little hollow for safety, for there were sometimes strong gusts of wind and he had no wish to see his precious food go bowling down the mountain. Then he lay down in the sun to rest after the strenuous climb. Heidi put her apronful of flowers in the same little hollow. Then she sat down beside Peter and looked around her. The valley below was bathed in sunlight. In front of them a snowclad mountain stood out against the blue sky and to the left of this was a huge mass of rock, with jagged twin peaks. Everything was very still. Only a

gentle breeze set the blue and yellow flowers nodding on their slender stems.

Peter fell asleep and the goats climbed about among the bushes. Heidi sat quite still, enjoying it all. She gazed so intently at the mountain peaks that soon they seemed to her to have faces and to be looking like old friends. Suddenly she heard a loud noise. Looking up, she saw an enormous bird, circling overhead with outstretched wings and croaking harshly as it flew. "Peter, Peter, wake up!" she cried. "Here's the hawk." Peter sat up and together they watched as the great bird soared higher and higher into the sky and finally disappeared over the gray peaks.

"Where's it gone?" asked Heidi, who had never seen a bird as big as that before and had watched its flight with great interest.

"Home to its nest," replied Peter.

"Does it live right up there? How wonderful! Why does it make such a noise?"

"Because it has to," explained Peter briefly.

"Let's climb up and see where it lives," she proposed.

"Oh, no, we won't! Even the goats can't climb as high as that, and don't forget Uncle told me to look after you," he said with marked disapproval. To Heidi's surprise he began whistling and shouting, but the goats recognized the familiar sounds and came toward him from all directions, though some lingered to nibble a tasty blade of grass, while others butted one another playfully. Heidi jumped up and ran among them, delighted to see them so obviously enjoying themselves. She spoke to each one, and every one was different and easily distinguishable from the others.

Meanwhile, Peter opened his bag and spread its contents out in a square on the ground, two large portions for Heidi and two smaller ones for himself. Then he filled the mug with milk from Daisy and placed it in the middle of the square. He called to

Heidi, but she was slower to come than the goats had been. She was so busy with her new playmates that she had ears and eyes for nothing else. He went on calling till his voice re-echoed from the rocks and at last she appeared. When she saw the meal laid out so invitingly, she skipped up and down with pleasure.

"Stop jigging about," said Peter, "it's dinnertime. Sit down and eat."

"Is the milk for me?"

"Yes, and those huge pieces of bread and cheese. I'll get you another mugful from Daisy when you've drunk that one. Then I'll have a drink myself."

"Where will you get yours from?" she inquired.

"From my own goat, Spot. Now start eating."

She drank the milk, but ate only a small piece of bread and passed the rest over to Peter, with the cheese. "You can have that," she said. "I've had enough." He looked at her in amazement for he had never in his life had any food to give away. At first he hesitated, thinking she must be joking, but she went on holding it out to him and finally put it on his knee. This convinced him that she really meant what she said, so he took it, nodded his thanks, and settled down to enjoy the feast. Heidi meanwhile sat watching the goats.

"What are they all called, Peter?" she asked presently.

Peter did not know a great deal, but this was a question he could answer without difficulty. He told her all the names, pointing to each animal in turn. She listened attentively and soon knew one from the other. Each had little tricks by which it could easily be recognized by anyone looking at them closely, as she was doing. Big Turk had strong horns, and was always trying to butt the others, so they kept out of his way as much as possible. The only one to answer him back was a frisky little kid called Finch, with sharp little horns, and Turk was generally too

astonished at such impudence to make a fight of it. Heidi was
particularly attracted to a little white goat called Snowflake, which
was bleating most pitifully. She had tried earlier to comfort it. Now
she ran up to it again, put her arm around its neck, and asked
fondly, "What's the matter, Snowflake? What are you crying for?"
At that, the goat nestled against her and stopped bleating.

Peter had not yet finished his meal, but he called out between
mouthfuls, "She's crying because her mother doesn't come up here
anymore. She's been sold to someone in Mayenfeld."

"Where's her grandmother then?"

"Hasn't got one."

"Or her grandfather?"

"Hasn't one."

"Poor Snowflake," said Heidi, hugging the little animal again.
"Don't cry anymore. I shall be up here every day now, and you
can always come to me if you feel lonely." Snowflake rubbed her
head on the little girl's shoulder, and seemed to be comforted.

Peter had now finished eating and came up to Heidi, who was
making fresh discoveries all the time. She noticed that Daisy and
Dusky seemed more independent than the other goats and carried
themselves with a sort of dignity. They led the way as the herd
went up to the bushes again. Some of them stopped here and
there to sample a tasty herb, others went straight up, leaping over
any small obstacles in their path. Turk was up to his tricks as
usual, but Daisy and Dusky ignored him completely and were
soon nibbling daintily at the leaves of the two thickest bushes.
Heidi watched them for some time. Then she turned to Peter, who
was lying full-length on the grass.

"Daisy and Dusky are the prettiest of all the goats," she said.

"I know. That's Uncle—he keeps them very clean and gives
them salt and he has a fine stall for them," he replied. Then he

suddenly jumped up and ran after his herd, with Heidi close behind, anxious not to miss anything. He had noticed that inquisitive little Finch was right at the edge of the ravine, where the ground fell away so steeply that if it went any farther, it might fall over, and would certainly break its legs. Peter stretched out his hands to catch hold of the little kid, but he slipped and fell, though he managed to grasp one of its legs, and Finch, highly indignant at such treatment, struggled wildly to get away. "Heidi, come here," called Peter, "come and help."

He couldn't get up unless he let go of Finch's leg, which he was nearly pulling out of its socket already. Heidi saw at once what to do and pulled up a handful of grass, which she held under Finch's nose.

"Come on, don't be silly," she said. "You don't want to fall down there and hurt yourself."

At that, the little goat turned around and ate the grass from Heidi's hand, and Peter was able to get up. He took hold of the cord, on which a little bell was hung around Finch's neck. Heidi took hold of it too, on the other side, and together they brought the runaway safely back to the herd. Then Peter took up his stick to give it a good beating, and, seeing what was coming, Finch tried to get out of the way.

"Don't beat him," pleaded Heidi. "See how frightened he is."

"He deserves it," Peter replied, raising his arm, but she caught hold of him and exclaimed, "No, don't do that! It will hurt him. Leave him alone!" She looked at him so fiercely that he was astonished and dropped the stick.

"I won't beat him if you'll give me some of your cheese again tomorrow," he said, feeling he ought to have some compensation after the fright the little goat had given him.

"You can have it all, tomorrow and every day," promised Heidi. "I won't want it. And I'll give you some of my bread as well, but then you must never beat Finch or Snowflake or any of them."

"It's all the same to me," said Peter, which was his way of saying that he promised. He let Finch go and he bounded back to the herd.

It was getting late and the setting sun spread a wonderful golden glow over the grass and the flowers, and the high peaks shone and sparkled. Heidi sat for a while, quietly enjoying the beautiful scene, then all at once she jumped up, crying, "Peter, Peter! A fire, a fire! The mountains are on fire and the snow and the sky, too. Look, the trees and the rocks are all burning, even up there by the hawk's nest. Everything's on fire!"

"It's always like this in the evening," Peter said calmly, whittling away at his stick. "It's not a fire."

"What is it then?" she cried, rushing about to look at the wonderful sight from all sides. "What is it, Peter?"

"It just happens," he said.

"Oh, just look, the mountains have gotten all rosy-red! Look at the one with the snow on top. What are their names, Peter?"

"Mountains don't have names," he answered.

"How pretty the rosy snow looks, and the red rocks. Oh dear," she added, after a pause, "now the color's going and everything's turning gray. Oh, it's all over." She sat down, looking as upset as if it was indeed the end of everything.

"It'll be the same again tomorrow," explained Peter. "Now it's time to go home." He whistled and called the goats together and they started the downward journey.

"Is it always like this up here?" asked Heidi hopefully.

"Usually."

"Will it be the same tomorrow?"

"Yes, it will," he assured her.

With this she was content, and as she had so much to think

about, she didn't say another wo̶̶̶̶̶ ̶̶̶̶̶ey reached the cabin and saw her grandfather sitting under ̶̶̶̶̶ ̶̶̶̶̶rees, on the seat he had fixed there so that he could watch̶ ̶̶or the return of his animals. The little girl ran toward him, followed by Daisy and Dusky, and Peter called, "Good night, Heidi. Come again tomorrow." She ran back to say good-bye and promised to go with him the next day.

Heidi

...rd till th...
...the fir... n...
Int... f...

I expect you've always thought that being a witch comes naturally. Not so, as Mildred Hubble quickly finds out. After only two days at Miss Cackle's Academy for Witches, she crashes her broomstick against the wall. Try as she might to ride it, she always seems to topple off. And have you ever heard of a witch who is scared of the dark? Well, Mildred is! But at least she is inventive and, when her cat cannot balance on her broomstick, she puts it in her satchel for the ride, much to her teacher Miss Hardbroom's fury. Tomorrow, all the first-year witches are having a potion test. What will Mildred make of that?

THE WORST WITCH

JILL MURPHY

The Potion Test

It was the morning of the potion test, and the girls were filing
into the potion lab, each hoping she had learned the right spell,
except for Ethel, who knew everything and never worried about
such matters.

"Come along, girls! Two to a cauldron!" barked Miss Hardbroom.
"Today we shall make a laughter potion. No textbooks to be
used—put that book away this *instant*, Mildred! Work quietly, and
when you have finished you may take a small sip of the mixture
to make sure it is correctly made. You may begin."

Maud and Mildred were sharing a cauldron, of course, but
unfortunately neither of them had learned that particular spell.

"I think I can remember it vaguely," whispered Maud. "Bits of
it, anyway." She began to sort through the ingredients that had
been laid out on each workbench.

When everything was stirred together in the cauldron, the bubbling liquid was bright pink. Mildred stared at it doubtfully.

"I'm sure it should be green," she said. "In fact I'm sure we should have put in a handful of pondweed-gathered-at-midnight."

"Are you *sure?*" asked Maud.

"Yes . . ." replied Mildred, not very definitely.

"*Absolutely* sure?" Maud asked again. "You know what happened last time."

"I'm *quite* sure," insisted Mildred. "Anyway, there's a handful of pondweed laid out on each bench. I'm positive we're supposed to put it in."

"Oh, all right," said Maud. "Go on, then. It can't do any harm."

Mildred grabbed the pondweed and dropped it into the mixture. They took turns stirring it for a few minutes until it began to turn dark green.

"What a horrid color," said Maud.

"Are you ready, girls?" asked Miss Hardbroom, rapping on her desk. "You should have been ready minutes ago. A laughter potion should be made quickly for use in an emergency."

Ethel was still working on the bench in front of Mildred, who stood on tiptoe to sneak a look at the color of Ethel's potion. To her horror, it was bright pink.

"Oh, no," Mildred thought, with a sinking feeling. "I wonder what potion we've made?"

Miss Hardbroom banged on the desk again.

"We shall now test the potion," she commanded. "Not too much, please. We don't want anyone hysterical."

Each pupil took a test tubeful of liquid and drank a little. At once shrieks of laughter rang through the room, especially from Ethel's bench where they had made the best potion of all and were laughing so much that tears rolled down their cheeks. The only two girls who weren't laughing were Mildred and Maud.

"Oh, dear," said Maud. "I feel most peculiar. Why aren't we laughing, Mil?"

"I have to tell you," confessed Mildred, "I think—" But before she had time to say any more, the two girls had disappeared!

"Cauldron number two!" snapped Miss Hardbroom. "You seem to have made the wrong spell."

"It was my fault," said Mildred's voice from behind the cauldron.

"That I do not doubt," Miss Hardbroom said sourly. "You had both better sit down until you reappear, and then, Mildred, perhaps a trip to Miss Cackle's office would do you some good. You can explain why I sent you."

Everyone had left the room by the time the two young witches finally began to reappear. This was a very slow process, with first the head and then the rest of the body becoming gradually visible.

"I'm sorry," said Mildred's head and shoulders.

"That's all right," said Maud's head. "I just wish you'd *think* a bit more. We had the right potion to start with."

"Sorry," mumbled Mildred again, then she began to laugh. "Hey, Maud, you do look funny with just your head showing!"

At once they both began to laugh, and soon they were best friends again.

"I suppose I'd better go and see Old Cackle now," said Mildred, when she had completely reappeared.

"I'll come with you to the door," offered Maud.

Miss Cackle was small and very fat, with short gray hair and green horn-rimmed glasses, which she usually wore pushed up on top of her head. She was the exact opposite of Miss Hardbroom, being absentminded in appearance and rather gentle by nature. The girls were not in the least bit afraid of her, whereas

Miss Hardbroom could reduce any of them to a miserable heap with just one word. Miss Cackle used a different technique. By always being friendly and pleased to see a pupil in her office, she made them feel embarrassed if they had something unpleasant to tell her, as Mildred nearly always had.

Mildred knocked at Miss Cackle's door, hoping she would be out. She wasn't.

"Come in!" called the familiar voice from inside.

Mildred opened the door and went in. Miss Cackle, glasses on her nose for once, was busily writing in a huge register. She looked up and peered over her spectacles.

"Ah, Mildred," she said pleasantly. "Come and sit down while I finish filling in this register."

Mildred closed the door and sat by Miss Cackle's desk.

"I wish she wasn't so pleased to see me," she thought.

Miss Cackle slammed the register shut and pushed her glasses onto the top of her head.

"Now, Mildred, what can I do for you?"

Mildred twisted her fingers together.

"Well, actually, Miss Cackle," she began slowly. "Miss Hardbroom sent me to see you because I made the wrong potion again."

The smile faded from the headmistress's face and she sighed, as if with deep disappointment. Mildred felt about an inch high.

"Really, Mildred," Miss Cackle said in a tired voice, "I have run out of things to say to you. Week after week you come here, sent by every member of staff in the school, and my words just seem to go straight in one ear and out of the other. You will never get the Witches' Higher Certificate if this appalling conduct continues. You must be the worst witch in the entire school. Whenever there's any trouble you are nearly always to be found at the bottom of it, and it's just not good enough, my dear. Now, what have you to say for yourself this time?"

"I don't really know, Miss Cackle," Mildred said humbly. "Everything I do just seems to go wrong, that's all. I don't mean to do it."

"Well, that's no excuse, is it?" said Miss Cackle. "Everyone else manages to live without causing an uproar wherever they go. You must pull yourself together, Mildred. I don't want to hear any more bad reports about you, do you understand?"

"Yes, Miss Cackle," said Mildred, in as sorry a voice as she could manage.

"Run along, then," said the headmistress, "and remember what I have said to you."

Maud was waiting in the corridor, eager to know what had been said, when her friend came out of the office.

"She's nice really," Mildred said. "Just told me all the usual things. She hates telling people off. I'll have to try to be better from now on. Come on, let's go and give the kittens another broomstick lesson."

Introduction

*Mary, Laura, and Baby Carrie live with their
parents, Black Susan the cat, and Jack the bulldog,
in a log house deep in the woods of Wisconsin.
The little girls spend their days helping Ma to churn
butter and prepare the wild beasts Pa hunts for
dinner, and growing vegetables in the garden.
In the wintertime, they stay all snug and cozy inside
the little house, playing games of make-believe in
the attic, making paper dolls, and listening to
Pa's wonderful stories about when he was a boy.
And the most thrilling time of all?
Why, Christmas, of course!*

LITTLE HOUSE IN THE BIG WOODS

LAURA INGALLS WILDER

Christmas

Christmas was coming.

The little log house was almost buried in snow. Great drifts were banked against the walls and windows, and in the morning when Pa opened the door, there was a wall of snow as high as Laura's head. Pa took the shovel and shoveled it away, and then he shoveled a path to the barn, where the horses and cows were snug and warm in their stalls.

The days were clear and bright. Laura and Mary stood on chairs by the window and looked out across the glittering snow at the glittering trees. Snow was piled all along their bare, dark branches, and it sparkled in the sunshine. Icicles hung from the eaves of the house to the snowbanks, great icicles as large at the top as Laura's arm. They were like glass and full of sharp lights.

Pa's breath hung in the air like smoke, when he came along

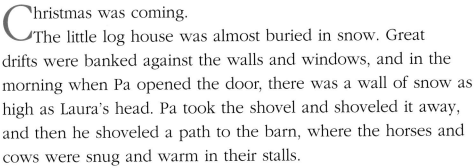

the path from the barn. He breathed it out in clouds and it froze in white frost on his mustache and beard.

When he came in, stamping the snow from his boots, and caught Laura up in a bear hug against his cold, big coat, his mustache was beaded with little drops of melting frost.

Every night he was busy, working on a large piece of board and two small pieces. He whittled them with his knife, he rubbed them with sandpaper and with the palm of his hand, until when Laura touched them they felt soft and smooth as silk.

Then with his sharp jackknife he worked at them, cutting the edges of the large one into little peaks and towers, with a large star curved on the very tallest point. He cut little holes through the wood. He cut the holes in shapes of windows, and the little stars, and crescent moons, and circles. All around them he carved tiny leaves, and flowers and birds.

One of the lovely boards he shaped in a lovely curve, and around its edges he carved leaves and flowers and stars, and through it he cut crescent moons and curlicues.

Around the edges of the smallest board he carved a tiny flowering vine.

He made the tiniest shavings, cutting very slowly and carefully, making whatever he thought would be pretty.

At last he had the pieces finished and one night he fit them together. When this was done, the large piece was a beautifully carved back for a smooth little shelf across its middle. The large star was at the very top of it. The curved piece supported the shelf underneath, and it was carved beautifully, too. And the little vine ran around the edge of the shelf.

Pa had made this bracket for a Christmas present for Ma. He hung it carefully against the log wall between the windows, and Ma stood her little china woman on the shelf.

The little china woman had a china bonnet on her head, and china curls hung against her china neck. Her china dress was laced across in front, and she wore a pale pink china apron and little gilt china shoes. She was beautiful, standing on the shelf with flowers and leaves and birds and moons carved all around her, and the large star at the very top.

Ma was busy all day long, cooking good things for Christmas. She baked salt-rising bread and rye'n'Injun bread, and Swedish crackers, and a huge pan of baked beans, with salt pork and molasses. She baked vinegar pies and dried-apple pies, and filled a big jar with cookies, and she let Laura and Mary lick the cake spoon.

One morning she boiled molasses and sugar together until they made a thick syrup, and Pa brought in two pans of clean, white snow from outdoors. Laura and Mary each had a pan, and Pa and Ma showed them how to pour the dark syrup in little streams on to the snow.

They made circles and curlicues and squiggledy things, and these hardened at once and were candy. Laura and Mary might eat one piece each, but the rest were saved for Christmas Day.

All this was done because Aunt Eliza and Uncle Peter and the cousins, Peter and Alice and Ella, were coming to spend Christmas.

The day before Christmas they came. Laura and Mary heard the gay ringing of sleigh bells, growing louder every moment, and then the big bobsled came out of the woods and drove up to the gate. Aunt Eliza and Uncle Peter and the cousins were in it, all covered up, under blankets and robes and buffalo skins.

They were wrapped up in so many coats and mufflers and veils and shawls that they looked like big, shapeless bundles.

When they all came in, the little house was full and running over. Black Susan ran out and hid in the barn, but Jack leaped in

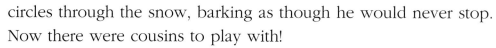
circles through the snow, barking as though he would never stop. Now there were cousins to play with!

As soon as Aunt Eliza had unwrapped them, Peter and Alice and Ella and Laura and Mary began to run and shout. At last Aunt Eliza told them to be quiet. Then Alice said:

"I'll tell you what let's do. Let's make pictures."

Alice said they must go outdoors to do it, and Ma thought it was too cold for Laura to play outdoors. But when she saw how disappointed Laura was, she said she might go, after all, for a little while. She put on Laura's coat and mittens and the warm cape with the hood, and wrapped a muffler around her neck, and let her go.

Laura had never had so much fun. All morning she played outdoors in the snow with Alice and Ella and Peter and Mary, making pictures. The way they did it was this:

Each one climbed up on a stump, and then all at once, holding their arms out wide, they fell off the stumps into the soft, deep snow. They fell flat on their faces. Then they tried to get up without spoiling the marks they made when they fell. If they did it well, there in the snow were five holes, shaped almost exactly like four little girls and a boy, arms and legs and all. They called these their pictures.

They played so hard all day that when night came they were too excited to sleep. But they must sleep, or Santa Claus would not come. So they hung their stockings by the fireplace, and said their prayers, and went to bed—Alice and Ella and Mary and Laura all in one big bed on the floor.

Peter had the trundle bed. Aunt Eliza and Uncle Peter were going to sleep in the big bed, and another bed was made on the attic floor for Pa and Ma. The buffalo robes and all the blankets had been brought in from Uncle Peter's sled, so there were enough covers for everybody.

· · ·

They lay there whispering till Ma said: "Charles, those children never will get to sleep unless you play for them." So Pa got his fiddle.

The room was still and warm and full of firelight. Ma's shadow, and Aunt Eliza's and Uncle Peter's were big and quivering on the walls in the flickering firelight, and Pa's fiddle sang merrily to itself.

It sang "Money Musk" and "The Red Heifer," "The Devil's Dream" and "Arkansas Traveler." And Laura went to sleep while Pa and the fiddle were both softly singing:

> *"My darling Nelly Gray, they have taken you away,*
> *And I'll never see my darling anymore . . . ."*

In the morning they all woke up almost at the same moment. They looked at their stockings, and something was in them. Santa Claus had been there. Alice and Ella and Laura in their red flannel nightgowns and Peter in his red flannel nightshirt, all ran shouting to see what he had brought.

In each stocking there was a pair of bright red mittens and there was a long flat stick of red-and-white-striped peppermint candy, all beautifully notched along the side.

They were all so happy they could hardly speak at first. They just looked with shining eyes at those lovely Christmas presents. But Laura was happiest of all. Laura had a rag doll.

She was a beautiful doll. She had a face of white cloth with black button eyes. A black pencil had made her eyebrows, and her cheeks and her mouth were red with the ink made from pokeberries. Her hair was black yarn that had been knitted and raveled, so that it was curly.

She had little red flannel stockings and little black cloth gaiters for shoes, and her dress was pretty pink and blue calico.

She was so beautiful that Laura could not say a word. She just held her tight and forgot everything else. She did not know that everyone was looking at her, till Aunt Eliza said:

"Did you ever see such big eyes!"

The other girls were not jealous that Laura had mittens, and candy, *and* a doll, because Laura was the littlest girl, except Baby Carrie and Aunt Eliza's little baby, Dolly Varden. The babies were too small for dolls. They were so small they did not even know about Santa Claus. They just put their fingers in their mouths and wriggled because of all the excitement.

Laura sat down on the edge of the bed and held her doll. She loved her red mittens and she loved the candy, but she loved her doll best of all. She named her Charlotte.

Then they all looked at each other's mittens, and tried on their own, and Peter bit a large piece out of his stick of candy, but Alice and Ella and Mary and Laura licked theirs, to make it last longer.

"Well, well!" Uncle Peter said. "Isn't there even one stocking with nothing but a switch in it? My, my, have you all been such good children?"

But they didn't believe Santa Claus could, really, have given any of them nothing but a switch. That happened to some children, but it couldn't happen to them. It was so hard to be good all the time, every day, for a whole year.

"You mustn't tease the children, Peter," Aunt Eliza said.

Ma said, "Laura, aren't you going to let the other girls hold your doll?" She meant, "Little girls must not be so selfish."

So Laura let Mary take the beautiful doll, and then Alice held her a minute, and then Ella. They smoothed the pretty dress and admired the red flannel stockings and the gaiters, and the curly woollen hair. But Laura was glad when at last Charlotte was safe in her arms again.

Pa and Uncle Peter each had a pair of new, warm mittens, knitted

in little squares of red and white. Ma and Aunt Eliza had made them.

Aunt Eliza had brought Ma a large red apple stuck full of cloves. How good it smelled! And it would not spoil, for so many cloves would keep it sound and sweet.

Ma gave Aunt Eliza a little needlebook she had made, with bits of silk for covers and soft white flannel leaves into which to stick the needles. The flannel would keep the needles from rusting.

They all admired Ma's beautiful bracket, and Aunt Eliza said that Uncle Peter had made one for her—of course, with different carving.

Santa Claus had not given them anything at all. Santa Claus did not give grown people presents, but that was not because they had not been good. Pa and Ma were good. It was because they were grown up, and grown people must give each other presents.

Then all the presents must be laid away for a little while. Peter went out with Pa and Uncle Peter to do the chores, and Alice and Ella helped Aunt Eliza make the beds, and Laura and Mary set the table, while Ma got breakfast.

For breakfast there were pancakes, and Ma made a pancake man for each one of the children. Ma called each one in turn to bring her plate, and each could stand by the stove and watch, while with the spoonful of batter Ma put on the arms and the legs and the head. It was exciting to watch her turn the whole little man over, quickly and carefully, on a hot griddle. When it was done, she put it smoking-hot on the plate.

Peter ate the head off his man, right away. But Alice and Ella and Mary and Laura ate theirs slowly in little bits, first the arms and legs and then the middle, saving the head for last.

Today the weather was so cold that they could not play outdoors, but there were the new mittens to admire, and the candy to lick. And they all sat on the floor together and looked at the pictures in the Bible, and the pictures of all kinds of animals

and birds in Pa's big green book. Laura kept Charlotte in her arms the whole time.

Then there was the Christmas dinner. Alice and Ella and Peter and Mary and Laura did not say a word at table, for they knew that children should be seen and not heard. But they did not need to ask for second helpings. Ma and Aunt Eliza kept their plates full and let them eat all the good things they could hold.

"Christmas comes but once a year," said Aunt Eliza.

Dinner was early, because Aunt Eliza, Uncle Peter, and the cousins had such a long way to go.

"Best the horses can do," Uncle Peter said. "We'll hardly make it home before dark."

So as soon as they had eaten dinner, Uncle Peter and Pa went to put the horses to the sled, while Ma and Aunt Eliza wrapped up the cousins.

They pulled heavy woolen stockings over the woolen stockings and the shoes they were already wearing. They put on mittens and coats and warm hoods and shawls, and wrapped mufflers around their necks and thick woolen veils over their faces. Ma slipped piping hot baked potatoes into their pockets to keep their fingers warm and Aunt Eliza's flatirons were hot on the stove, ready to put at their feet in the sled. The blankets and the quilts and the buffalo robes were warmed, too.

So they all got into the big bobsled, cozy and warm, and Pa tucked the last robe well in around them.

"Good-bye! Good-bye!" they called, and off they went, the horses trotting gaily and the sleigh bells ringing.

In just a little while the merry sound of the bells was gone, and Christmas was over. But what a happy Christmas it had been!

Introduction

We all sing, "We're off to see the Wizard, the wonderful
Wizard of Oz . . . ," but how many of us know about
Dorothy's adventure in the magical land of Oz with her little
dog Toto? It all begins when a rampaging cyclone sweeps
across the plains of Kansas, whirls her little wooden house
high into the air, and sets it down in the middle of a strange
country of marvelous beauty. All Dorothy can think about is
finding her way back home to Kansas, to be with Aunt Em
and Uncle Harry. Four funny little people called Munchkins
approach her and suggest that the Wizard of Oz might help,
so off she sets, following the road of yellow brick, to his
palace in the Emerald City. On the way she is joined by the
Scarecrow, who longs for a brain, the Tin Woodman, who
wants a heart, and the Cowardly Lion, who wishes he were
brave. Perhaps the Wizard will be able to help them, too.
They have all manner of mysterious adventures along the
yellow brick road, but as they get closer to the Emerald City,
the fulfillment of their dreams still seems far away.

THE WIZARD OF OZ

L. FRANK BAUM

The Guardian of the Gates

"We must journey on until we find the road of yellow brick again," said Dorothy; "and then we can keep on to the Emerald City."

So, the Lion being fully refreshed, and feeling quite himself again, they all started upon the journey, greatly enjoying the walk through the soft, fresh grass; and it was not long before they reached the road of yellow brick and turned again toward the Emerald City where the great Oz dwelled.

The road was smooth and well paved now, and the country about was beautiful, so that the travelers rejoiced in leaving the forest far behind, and with it the many dangers they had met in its gloomy shades. Once more they could see fences built beside the road; but these were painted green, and when they came to a small house, in which a farmer evidently lived, that also was painted green. They passed by several of these houses during the afternoon, and sometimes people came to the doors and looked at them as if they would like to ask questions; but no one came near them nor spoke to them because of the great Lion, of which they were much afraid. The people were all dressed in clothing of a lovely emerald-green color and wore peaked hats like those of the Munchkins.

"This must be the Land of Oz," said Dorothy, "and we are surely getting near the Emerald City."

"Yes," answered the Scarecrow. "Everything is green here, while in the country of the Munchkins blue was the favorite color. But the people do not seem to be as friendly as the Munchkins and I'm afraid we shall be unable to find a place to pass the night."

"I should like something to eat besides fruit," said the girl, "and I'm sure Toto is nearly starved. Let us stop at the next house and talk to the people."

So, when they came to a good-sized farmhouse, Dorothy walked boldly up to the door and knocked.

A woman opened it just far enough to look out, and said, "What do you want, child, and why is that great Lion with you?"

"We wish to pass the night with you, if you will allow us," answered Dorothy; "and the Lion is my friend and comrade, and would not hurt you for the world."

"Is he tame?" asked the woman, opening the door a little wider.

"Oh, yes," said the girl, "and he is a great coward, too; so that he will be more afraid of you than you are of him."

"Well," said the woman, after thinking it over and taking another peep at the Lion, "if that is the case you may come in, and I will give you some supper and a place to sleep."

So they entered the house, where there were, besides the woman, two children and a man. The man had hurt his leg, and was lying on the couch in a corner. They seemed greatly surprised to see so strange a company, and while the woman was busy laying the table the man asked:

"Where are you all going?"

"To the Emerald City," said Dorothy, "to see the Great Oz."

"Oh, indeed!" exclaimed the man. "Are you sure that Oz will see you?"

"Why not?" she replied.

"Why, it is said that he never lets anyone come into his presence. I have been to the Emerald City many times, and it is a beautiful and wonderful place; but I have never been permitted to see the Great Oz, nor do I know of any living person who has seen him."

"Does he never go out?" asked the Scarecrow.

"Never. He sits day after day in the great throne room of his palace, and even those who wait upon him do not see him face to face."

"What is he like?" asked the girl.

"That is hard to tell," said the man thoughtfully. "You see, Oz is a great Wizard, and can take on any form he wishes. So that some say he looks like a bird; and some say he looks like an elephant; and some say he looks like a cat. To others he appears as a beautiful fairy, or a brownie, or in any form that pleases him. But who the real Oz is, when he is in his own form, no living person can tell."

"That is very strange," said Dorothy, "but we must try, in some way, to see him, or we shall have made our journey for nothing."

"Why do you wish to see the terrible Oz?" asked the man.

"I want him to give me a brain," said the Scarecrow eagerly.

"Oh, Oz could do that easily enough," declared the man. "He has more brains than he needs."

"And I want him to give me a heart," said the Tin Woodman.

"That will not trouble him," continued the man, "for Oz has a large collection of hearts, of all sizes and shapes."

"And I want him to give me courage," said the Cowardly Lion.

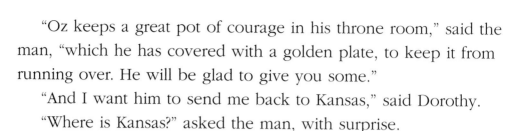

"Oz keeps a great pot of courage in his throne room," said the man, "which he has covered with a golden plate, to keep it from running over. He will be glad to give you some."

"And I want him to send me back to Kansas," said Dorothy.

"Where is Kansas?" asked the man, with surprise.

"I don't know," replied Dorothy sorrowfully, "but it is my home, and I'm sure it's somewhere."

"Very likely. Well, Oz can do anything; so I suppose he will find Kansas for you. But first you must get to see him, and that will be a hard task; for the Great Wizard does not like to see anyone, and he usually has his own way. But what do *you* want?" he continued, speaking to Toto. Toto only wagged his tail; for, strange to say, he could not speak.

The woman now called to them that supper was ready, so they gathered around the table and Dorothy ate some delicious porridge and a dish of scrambled eggs and a plate of nice white bread, and enjoyed her meal. The Lion ate some of the porridge, but did not care for it, saying it was made from oats and oats were food for horses, not for lions. The Scarecrow and the Tin Woodman ate nothing at all. Toto ate a little of everything, and was glad to get a good supper again.

The woman now gave Dorothy a bed to sleep in, and Toto lay down beside her, while the Lion guarded the door of her room so she might not be disturbed. The Scarecrow and the Tin Woodman stood up in a corner and kept quiet all night, although of course they could not sleep.

The next morning, as soon as the sun was up, they started on their way, and soon saw a beautiful green glow in the sky just before them.

"That must be the Emerald City," said Dorothy.

As they walked on, the green glow became brighter and

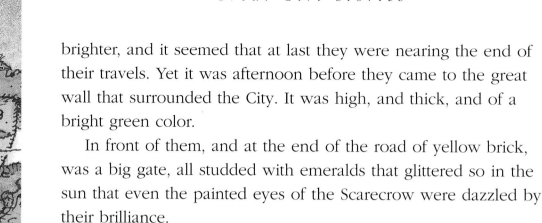

brighter, and it seemed that at last they were nearing the end of their travels. Yet it was afternoon before they came to the great wall that surrounded the City. It was high, and thick, and of a bright green color.

In front of them, and at the end of the road of yellow brick, was a big gate, all studded with emeralds that glittered so in the sun that even the painted eyes of the Scarecrow were dazzled by their brilliance.

There was a bell beside the gate, and Dorothy pushed the button and heard a silvery tinkle sound within. Then the big gate swung slowly open, and they all passed through and found themselves in a high arched room, the walls of which glistened with countless emeralds.

Before them stood a little man about the same size as the Munchkins. He was clothed all in green, from his head to his feet, and even his skin was of a greenish tint. At his side was a large green box.

When he saw Dorothy and her companions the man asked, "What do you wish in the Emerald City?"

"We came here to see the Great Oz," said Dorothy.

The man was so surprised at this answer that he sat down to think it over.

"It has been many years since anyone asked me to see Oz," he said, shaking his head in perplexity. "He is powerful and terrible, and if you come on an idle or foolish errand to bother the wise reflections of the Great Wizard, he might be angry and destroy you all in an instant."

"But it is not a foolish errand, nor an idle one," replied the Scarecrow; "it is important. And we have been told that Oz is a good Wizard."

"So he is," said the green man; "and he rules the Emerald City wisely and well. But to those who are not honest, or who approach him from curiosity, he is most terrible, and few have ever dared ask to see his face. I am the Guardian of the Gates, and since you demand to see the Great Oz I must take you to his palace. But first you must put on the spectacles."

"Why?" asked Dorothy.

"Because if you did not wear spectacles the brightness and the glory of the Emerald City would blind you. Even those who live in the City must wear spectacles night and day. They are all locked on, for Oz so ordered it when the City was first built, and I have the only key that will unlock them."

He opened the big box, and Dorothy saw that it was filled with spectacles of every size and shape. All of them had green glasses in them. The Guardian of the Gates found a pair that would just fit Dorothy and put them over her eyes. There were two golden bands fastened to them that passed around the back of her head, where they were locked together by a little key that was at the end of a chain the Guardian of the Gates wore around his neck. When they were on, Dorothy could not take them off had she wished, but of course she did not wish to be blinded by the glare of the Emerald City, so she said nothing.

Then the green man fitted spectacles for the Scarecrow and the Tin Woodman and the Lion, and even little Toto; and all were locked fast with the key.

Then the Guardian of the Gates put on his own glasses and told them he was ready to show them to the palace. Taking a big golden key from a peg on the wall, he opened another gate, and they all followed him through the portal into the streets of the Emerald City.

Introduction

Coming to a boarding school in England from her home in India is a big leap for Sara Crewe. She is only seven but already she feels as if she has lived a long, long time. Driving through the gloomy London streets with her father, they arrive at the dull red-brick building that is to be her home. MISS MINCHIN Select Seminary for Young Ladies *reads the sign, and Sara's heart sinks. It is not school that Sara fears, for she is always sitting with her nose in a book, and lessons are not a problem for her. But saying good-bye to her beloved father as he sets off for their beautiful home back in Bombay—that is the hardest thing of all. However, with her new doll, Emily, at her side, she goes into battle, determined to make her father proud of her.*

A LITTLE PRINCESS

FRANCES HODGSON BURNETT

A French Lesson

When Sara entered the schoolroom the next morning everybody looked at her with wide, interested eyes. By that time every pupil—from Lavinia Herbert, who was nearly thirteen and felt quite grown up, to Lottie Legh, who was only just four and the baby of the school—had heard a great deal about her. They knew very certainly that she was Miss Minchin's show pupil and was considered a credit to the establishment. One or two of them had even caught a glimpse of her French maid, Mariette, who had arrived the evening before. Lavinia had managed to pass Sara's room when the door was open, and had seen Mariette opening a box which had arrived late from some ship.

"It was full of petticoats with lace frills on them—frills and frills," she whispered to her friend Jessie as she bent over her geography. "I saw her shaking them out. I heard Miss Minchin say to Miss Amelia that her clothes were so grand that they were

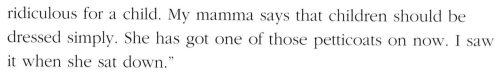

ridiculous for a child. My mamma says that children should be dressed simply. She has got one of those petticoats on now. I saw it when she sat down."

"She has silk stockings on!" whispered Jessie, bending over her geography also. "And what little feet! I never saw such little feet."

"Oh," sniffed Lavinia spitefully, "that is the way her slippers are made. My mamma says that even big feet can be made to look small if you have a clever shoemaker. I don't think she is pretty at all. Her eyes are such a queer color."

"She isn't pretty as other pretty people are," said Jessie, stealing a glance across the room, "but she makes you want to look at her again. She has tremendously long eyelashes, but her eyes are almost green."

Sara was sitting quietly in her seat, waiting to be told what to do. She had been placed near Miss Minchin's desk. She was not abashed at all by the many pairs of eyes watching her. She was interested, and looked back quietly at the children who looked at her. She wondered what they were thinking of, and if they liked Miss Minchin, and if they cared for their lessons, and if any of them had a papa at all like her own. She had had a long talk with Emily about her papa that morning.

"He is on the sea now, Emily," she had said. "We must be very great friends to each other and tell each other things. Emily, look at me. You have the nicest eyes I ever saw—but I wish you could speak."

She was a child full of imaginings and whimsical thoughts, and one of her fancies was that there would be a great deal of comfort in even pretending that Emily was alive and really heard and understood. After Mariette had dressed her in her dark-blue school-room frock and tied her hair with a dark-blue ribbon, she went to Emily, who sat in a chair of her own, and gave her a book.

"You can read that while I am downstairs," she said; and seeing Mariette looking at her curiously, she spoke to her with a serious little face.

"What I believe about dolls," she said, "is that they can do things they will not let us know about. Perhaps, really, Emily can read and talk and walk, but she will only do it when people are out of the room. That is her secret. You see, if people knew that dolls could do things, they would make them work. So, perhaps they have promised each other to keep it a secret. If you stay in the room, Emily will just sit there and stare; but if you go out, she will begin to read, perhaps, or go and look out of the window. Then if she heard either of us coming, she would just run back and jump into her chair and pretend she had been there all the time."

"*Comme elle est drôle!*" Mariette said to herself, and when she went downstairs she told the head housemaid about it. But she had already begun to like this odd little girl who had such an

intelligent small face and such perfect manners. She had taken care of children before who were not so polite. Sara was a very fine little person, and had a gentle, appreciative way of saying: "If you please, Mariette," "Thank you, Mariette," which was very charming. Mariette told the head housemaid that she thanked her as if she was thanking a lady.

"*Elle a l'air d'une princesse, cette petite,*" she said. Indeed, she was very much pleased with her new little mistress and liked her place greatly.

After Sara had sat in her seat in the schoolroom for a few minutes, being looked at by the pupils, Miss Minchin rapped in a dignified manner upon her desk.

"Young ladies," she said, "I wish to introduce you to your new companion." All the little girls rose in their places, and Sara rose also. "I shall expect you all to be very agreeable to Miss Crewe; she has just come to us from a great distance—in fact, from India. As soon as lessons are over you must make each other's acquaintance."

The pupils bowed ceremoniously, and Sara made a little curtsy, and then they sat down and looked at each other again.

"Sara," said Miss Minchin in her schoolroom manner, "come here to me."

She had taken a book from the desk and was turning over its leaves. Sara went to her politely.

"As your papa has engaged a French maid for you," she began, "I conclude that he wishes you to make a special study of the French language."

Sara felt a little awkward.

"I think he engaged her," she said, "because he—he thought I would like her, Miss Minchin."

"I am afraid," said Miss Minchin, with a slightly sour smile, "that you have been a very spoiled little girl and always imagine that things are done because you like them. My impression is that your papa wishes you to learn French."

If Sara had been older or less punctilious about being quite polite to people, she could have explained herself in a very few words. But, as it was, she felt a flush rising on her cheeks. Miss Minchin was a very severe and imposing person, and she seemed so absolutely sure that Sara knew nothing whatever of French that she felt as if it would be almost rude to correct her. The truth was that Sara could not remember the time when she had not seemed to know French. Her father had often spoken it to her when she had been a baby. Her mother had been a Frenchwoman, and Captain Crewe had loved her language, so it happened that Sara had always heard and been familiar with it.

"I—I have never really learned French, but—but—" she began, trying shyly to make herself clear.

One of Miss Minchin's chief secret annoyances was that she did not speak French herself, and was desirous of concealing the irritating fact. She, therefore, had no intention of discussing the matter and laying herself open to innocent questioning by a new little pupil.

"That is enough," she said with polite tartness. "If you have not learned, you must begin at once. The French master, Monsieur Dufarge, will be here in a few minutes. Take this book and look at it until he arrives."

Sara's cheeks felt warm. She went back to her seat and opened the book. She looked at the first page with a grave face. She knew it would be rude to smile, and she was very determined not to be rude. But it was very odd to find herself expected to study a page which told her that "*le père*" meant "the father," and "*la mère*" meant "the mother."

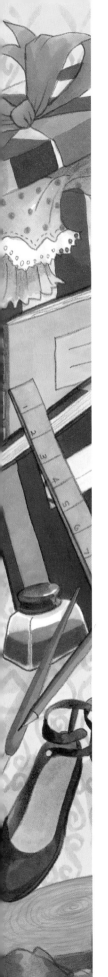

Miss Minchin glanced towards her scrutinizingly.

"You look rather cross, Sara," she said. "I am sorry you do not like the idea of learning French."

"I am very fond of it," answered Sara, thinking she would try again; "but—"

"You must not say 'but' when you are told to do things," said Miss Minchin. "Look at your book again."

And Sara did so, and did not smile, even when she found that "*le fils*" meant "the son," and "*le frère*" meant "the brother."

"When Monsieur Dufarge comes," she thought, "I can make him understand."

Monsieur Dufarge arrived very shortly afterward. He was a very nice, intelligent, middle-aged Frenchman, and he looked interested when his eyes fell upon Sara trying politely to seem absorbed in her little book of phrases.

"Is this a new pupil for me, madame?" he said to Miss Minchin. "I hope that is my good fortune."

"Her papa—Captain Crewe—is very anxious that she should begin the language. But I am afraid she has a childish prejudice against it. She does not seem to wish to learn," said Miss Minchin.

"I am sorry of that, mademoiselle," he said kindly to Sara. "Perhaps, when we begin to study together, I may show you that it is a charming tongue."

Little Sara rose in her seat. She was beginning to feel rather desperate, as if she were almost in disgrace. She looked up into Monsieur Dufarge's face with her big, green-gray eyes, and they were quite innocently appealing. She began to explain quite simply in pretty and fluent French. Madame had not understood. She had not learned French exactly—not out of books—but her papa and other people had always spoken it to her, and she had read it and written it as she had read and written English. Her papa loved it, and she loved it because he did. Her dear mamma, who had died when she was born, had been French. She would be glad to learn anything monsieur would teach her, but what she had tried to explain to madame was that she already knew the words in this book—and she held out the little book of phrases.

When she began to speak Miss Minchin started quite violently and sat staring at her over her eyeglasses, almost indignantly, until she had finished. Monsieur Dufarge began to smile, and his smile was one of great pleasure. To hear this pretty childish voice speaking his own language so simply and charmingly made him feel almost as if he were in his native land—which on dark, foggy days in London sometimes seemed worlds away. When she had finished, he took the phrasebook from her, with a look almost affectionate. But he spoke to Miss Minchin.

"Ah, madame," he said, "there is not much I can teach her. She has not *learned* French; she *is* French. Her accent is exquisite."

"You ought to have told me," exclaimed Miss Minchin, much mortified, turning on Sara.

"I—I tried," said Sara. "I—I suppose I did not begin right."

Miss Minchin knew she had tried, and that it had not been her fault that she was not allowed to explain. And when she saw that the pupils had been listening, and that Lavinia and Jessie were giggling behind their French grammars, she felt infuriated.

"Silence, young ladies!" she said severely, rapping upon the desk. "Silence at once!"

And she began from that minute to feel rather a grudge against her show pupil.

Introduction

Matilda is an exceptional child. She is only five, yet she can do complicated mathematics and has read grown-up books by Charles Dickens and Jane Austen—things that her older brother Michael can't do. But her unspeakably dreadful parents show no interest in their daughter's brilliance. Matilda tries to give them a dose of their own medicine: she pours superglue into her father's hat, and hides a talking parrot up the chimney to make them think a burglar is in the house. This is briefly satisfactory, but it is too much to hope that her parents will be taught a permanent lesson. Just look what happens when Matilda's quicksilver mathematical brain gets going.

MATILDA

ROALD DAHL

Arithmetic

Matilda longed for her parents to be good and loving and understanding and honorable and intelligent. The fact that they were none of these things was something she had to put up with. It was not easy to do so. But the new game she had invented of punishing one or both of them each time they were beastly to her made her life more or less bearable.

Being very small and very young, the only power Matilda had over anyone in her family was brainpower. For sheer cleverness she could run rings around them all. But the fact remained that any five-year-old girl in any family was always obliged to do as she was told, however asinine the orders might be. Thus she was always forced to eat her evening meals out of TV dinner trays in front of the dreaded box. She always had to stay alone on weekday afternoons, and whenever she was told to shut up, she had to shut up.

Her safety valve, the thing that prevented her from going round
the bend, was the fun of devising and dishing out these splendid
punishments, and the lovely thing was that they seemed to work,
at any rate for short periods. The father in particular became less
cocky and unbearable for several days after receiving a dose of
Matilda's magic medicine.

The parrot-in-the-chimney affair quite definitely cooled both
parents down a lot and for over a week they were comparatively
civil to their small daughter. But alas, this couldn't last. The next
flare-up came one evening in the sitting room. Mr. Wormwood had

just returned from work. Matilda and her brother were sitting quietly on the sofa waiting for their mother to bring in the TV dinners on a tray. The television had not yet been switched on.

In came Mr. Wormwood in a loud checked suit and a yellow tie. The appalling broad check of the jacket and trousers almost blinded the onlooker. He looked like a low-grade bookmaker dressed up for his daughter's wedding, and he was clearly very pleased with himself this evening. He sat down in an armchair and rubbed his hands together and addressed his son in a loud voice. "Well, my boy," he said, "your father's had a most

successful day. He is a lot richer tonight than he was this morning. He has sold no less than five cars, each one at a tidy profit. Sawdust in the gearboxes, the electric drill on the speedometer cables, a splash of paint here and there, and a few other clever little tricks and the idiots were all falling over themselves to buy."

He fished a bit of paper from his pocket and studied it. "Listen boy," he said, addressing the son and ignoring Matilda, "seeing as you'll be going into this business with me one day, you've got to know how to add up the profits you make at the end of each day. Go and get yourself a pad and a pencil and let's see how clever you are."

The son obediently left the room and returned with the writing materials.

"Write down these figures," the father said, reading from his bit of paper. "Car number one was bought by me for two hundred and seventy-eight pounds and sold for one thousand four hundred and twenty-five. Got that?"

The ten-year-old boy wrote the two separate amounts down slowly and carefully.

"Car number two," the father went on, "cost me one hundred and eighteen pounds and sold for seven hundred and sixty. Got it?"

"Yes, Dad," the son said. "I've got that."

"Car number three cost one hundred and eleven pounds and sold for nine hundred and ninety-nine pounds and fifty pence."

"Say that again," the son said. "How much did it sell for?"

"Nine hundred and ninety-nine pounds and fifty pence," the father said. "And that, by the way, is another of my nifty little tricks to diddle the customer. Never ask for a big round figure. Always go just below it. Never say one thousand pounds.

Always say nine hundred and ninety-nine fifty. It sounds much less, but it isn't. Clever, isn't it?"

"Very," the son said. "You're brilliant, Dad."

"Car number four cost eighty-six pounds—a real wreck that was—and sold for six hundred and ninety-nine pounds fifty."

"Not too fast," the son said, writing the numbers down. "Right. I've got it."

"Car number five cost six hundred and thirty-seven pounds and sold for sixteen hundred and forty-nine fifty. You got all those figures written down, Son?"

"Yes, Daddy," the boy said, crouching over his pad and carefully writing.

"Very well," the father said. "Now work out the profit I made on each of the five cars and add up the total. Then you'll be able to tell me how much money your rather brilliant father made altogether today."

"That's a lot of sums," the boy said.

"Of course it's a lot of sums," the father answered. "But when you're in big business like I am, you've got to be hot stuff at arithmetic. I've practically got a computer inside my head. It took me less than ten minutes to work the whole thing out."

"You mean you did it in your head, Dad?" the son asked, goggling.

"Well, not exactly," the father said. "Nobody could do that. But it didn't take me long. When you're finished, tell me what you think my profit was for the day. I've got the final total written down here and I'll tell you if you're right."

Matilda said quietly, "Dad, you made exactly four thousand three hundred and three pounds and fifty pence altogether."

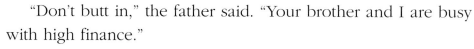
"Don't butt in," the father said. "Your brother and I are busy with high finance."

"But Dad . . ."

"Shut up," the father said. "Stop guessing and trying to be clever."

"Look at your answer, Dad," Matilda said gently. "If you've done it right it ought to be four thousand three hundred and three pounds and fifty pence. Is that what you've got, Dad?"

The father glanced down at the paper in his hand. He seemed to stiffen. He became very quiet. There was a silence. Then he said, "Say that again."

"Four thousand three hundred and three pounds fifty," Matilda said.

There was another silence. The father's face was beginning to go dark red.

"I'm sure it's right," Matilda said.

"You . . . you little cheat!" the father suddenly shouted, pointing at her with his finger. "You looked at my bit of paper! You read it off from what I've got written here!"

"Daddy, I'm the other side of the room," Matilda said. "How could I possibly see it?"

"Don't give me that rubbish!" the father shouted. "Of course you looked! You must have looked! No one in the world could give the right answer just like that, especially a girl! You're a little cheat, madam, that's what you are! A cheat and a liar!"

At that point, the mother came in carrying a large tray on which were the four suppers.

This time it was fish and chips, which Mrs. Wormwood had picked up in the fish and chip shop on her way home from bingo. It seemed that bingo afternoons left her so exhausted both physically and emotionally that she never had enough energy left to cook an evening meal. So if it wasn't TV dinners it had to be fish and chips. "What are you looking so red in the face about, Harry?" she said as she put the tray down on the coffee table.

"Your daughter's a cheat and a liar," the father said, taking his plate of fish and placing it on his knees. "Turn the telly on and let's not have any more talk."

Introduction

There are not many girls whose names have gone into everyday language: to call someone a Pollyanna means they are endlessly optimistic, always looking on the very brightest side of things. When the orphaned Pollyanna goes to stay with her stern aunt, Miss Polly Harrington, she is very excited, although Miss Polly's maid, Nancy, and the gardener's son, Timothy, both worry about how she will settle in in her new home. But Pollyanna's joy and enthusiasm are such that when she arrives, she does not notice Miss Polly's chilly greeting and rejoices at her luck at being in the big white house with the green shutters. Pollyanna is given an attic room, where there are no screens to keep out insects when the windows are open. One particularly hot night, Aunt Polly insists that the windows be kept closed to keep out flies—but Pollyanna has the answer to keeping cool.

POLLYANNA

ELEANOR H. PORTER

Pollyanna and Punishments

At half past eight Pollyanna went up to bed. The screens had not yet come, and the close little room was like an oven. With longing eyes Pollyanna looked at the two fast-closed windows—but she did not raise them. She undressed, folded her clothes neatly, said her prayers, blew out her candle, and climbed into bed.

Just how long she lay in sleepless misery, tossing from side to side of the hot little cot, she did not know; but it seemed to her that it must have been hours before she finally slipped out of bed, felt her way across the room and opened her door.

Out in the main attic all was velvet blackness save where the moon flung a path of silver halfway across the floor from the east dormer window. With a resolute ignoring of that fearsome darkness to the right and to the left, Pollyanna drew a quick breath and pattered straight into that silvery path, and on to the window.

She had hoped, vaguely, that this window might have a screen, but it did not. Outside, however, there was a wide world of fairylike beauty, and there was, too, she knew, fresh, sweet air that would feel so good to hot cheeks and hands!

As she stepped nearer and peered longingly out, she saw something else; she saw, only a little way below the window, the wide, flat tin roof of Miss Polly's sun parlor built over the *porte-cochère*. The sight filled her with longing. If only, now, she were out there!

Fearfully she looked behind her. Back there, somewhere, were her hot little room and her still hotter bed; but between her and them lay a horrid desert of blackness across which one must feel one's way with outstretched, shrinking arms; while before her, out on the sun parlor roof, were the moonlight and the cool, sweet night air.

If only her bed were out there! And folks did sleep out-of-doors. Joel Hartley at home, who was so sick with consumption, *had* to sleep out-of-doors.

Suddenly Pollyanna remembered that she had seen near this
attic window a row of long white bags hanging from nails. Nancy
had said they contained the winter clothing, put away for the
summer. A little fearfully now, Pollyanna felt her way to these
bags, selected a nice fat soft one (it contained Miss Polly's sealskin
coat) for a bed; and a thinner one to be doubled up for a pillow,
and still another (which was so thin it seemed almost empty) for a
covering. Thus equipped, Pollyanna in high glee pattered to the
moonlit window again, raised the sash, stuffed the burden through
to the roof below, then let herself down after it, closing the
window carefully behind her—Pollyanna had not forgotten those
flies with their marvelous feet that carried things.

How deliciously cool it was! Pollyanna quite danced up and
down with delight, drawing in long, full breaths of the refreshing
air. The tin roof under her feet crackled with little resounding
snaps that Pollyanna rather liked. She walked, indeed, two or three
times back and forth from end to end—it gave her such a pleasant
sensation of airy space after her hot little room; and the roof was
so broad and flat that she had no fear of falling off. Finally, with a
sigh of content, she curled herself up on the sealskin-coat mattress,
arranged one bag for a pillow and the other for a covering, and
settled herself to sleep.

"I'm so glad now that the screens didn't come," she murmured,
blinking up at the stars; "else I couldn't have had this!"

Downstairs in Miss Polly's room next to the sun parlor,
Miss Polly herself was hurrying into dressing gown and slippers,
her face white and frightened. A minute before she had been
telephoning in a shaking voice to Timothy.

"Come up quick!—you and your father. Bring lanterns.
Somebody is on the roof of the sun parlor. He must have climbed
up the rose trellis or somewhere, and of course he can get right

into the house through the east window in the attic. I have locked the attic door down here—but hurry, quick!"

Some time later, Pollyanna, just dropping off to sleep, was startled by a lantern flash, and a trio of amazed ejaculations. She opened her eyes to find Timothy at the top of a ladder near her, Old Tom just getting through the window, and her aunt peering out at her from behind him.

"Pollyanna, what does this mean?" cried Aunt Polly then.

Pollyanna blinked sleepy eyes and sat up.

"Why, Mr. Tom—Aunt Polly!" she stammered. "Don't look so scared! It isn't that I've got the consumption, you know, like Joel Hartley. It's only that I was so hot—in there. But I shut the window, Aunt Polly, so the flies couldn't carry those germ-things in."

Timothy disappeared suddenly down the ladder. Old Tom, with almost equal precipitation, handed his lantern to Miss Polly, and followed his son. Miss Polly bit her lip hard—until the men were gone, then she said sternly:

"Pollyanna, hand those things to me at once and come in here. Of all the extraordinary children!" she ejaculated a little later, as, with Pollyanna by her side, and the lantern in her hand, she turned back into the attic.

To Pollyanna the air was all the more stifling after that cool breath of the out-of-doors: but she did not complain. She only drew a long, quivering sigh.

At the top of the stairs Miss Polly jerked out crisply:

"For the rest of the night, Pollyanna, you are to sleep in my bed with me. The screens will be here tomorrow, but until then I consider it my duty to keep you where you are."

Pollyanna drew in her breath.

"With you?—in your bed?" she cried rapturously. "Oh, Aunt Polly, Aunt Polly, how perfectly lovely of you! And when I've so wanted to sleep with someone some time—someone that belonged to me, you know; not a Ladies' Aider. I've *had* them. My! I reckon I am glad now those screens didn't come! Wouldn't you be?"

There was no reply. Miss Polly was stalking on ahead. Miss Polly, to tell the truth, was feeling curiously helpless. For the third time since Pollyanna's arrival, Miss Polly was punishing Pollyanna—and for the third time she was being confronted with the amazing fact that her punishment was being taken as a special reward of merit. No wonder Miss Polly was feeling curiously helpless.

Introduction

Have you ever wanted to do extraordinary things
and to say the first thing that comes into your head,
no matter how impossibly silly? Well, for nine-year-old
Pippi with her red hair and peculiar clothes,
anything and everything is possible. A thoroughly
independent spirit, Pippi lives alone in a cottage in
Sweden with her horse and a monkey, and has the
wildest adventures imaginable. Here she is, with
her friends Tommy and Annika, on her very first
visit to the circus.

PIPPI LONGSTOCKING

ASTRID LINDGREN

Pippi Goes to the Circus

There was a crowd of people outside the circus tent, and in front of the ticket window stood a long line. By and by it was Pippi's turn. She stuck her head through the window, looked hard at the dear old lady who sat there, and said, "How much does it cost to look at *you?*"

The old lady was from a foreign country, so she didn't understand what Pippi meant. She answered, "Liddle girl, it is costink vive crones the front rows and dree crones the back rows and wan crones the zdandinkroom."

"I see," said Pippi. "But you must promise that you'll walk on the rope, too."

Now Tommy stepped in and said that Pippi would have a ticket for the back rows. Pippi gave a gold piece to the old lady and she looked at it suspiciously. She bit it, too, to see if it was real. At last she was convinced that it really was gold, and Pippi got her ticket. She got a great many silver coins in change as well.

"What do I want with all that nasty little white money?" said Pippi crossly. "Keep it. I'll look at you twice instead. From the zdandinkroom."

So, as Pippi absolutely didn't want any money back, the lady changed her ticket for a front row one, and gave Tommy and Annika front row tickets as well, without their having to add any money of their own. In this way, Pippi and Tommy and Annika came to sit on some very fine red chairs by the ringside. Tommy and Annika turned around several times in order to wave to their schoolmates, who sat much farther away.

"*This* is a queer hut," said Pippi, looking about her with wonder. "But they've spilled sawdust on the floor, I see. Not that I'm fussy, but it *does* look a bit untidy."

Tommy explained to Pippi that there was always sawdust in circus rings for the horses to run on.

On a platform sat the circus musicians, and they suddenly began to play a rousing march. Pippi clapped her hands wildly and jumped up and down in her chair with delight.

"Does it cost something to listen, too, or can you do that free?" she wondered.

Just then, the curtain was pulled back from the artistes' entrance, and the ringmaster, dressed in black and with a whip in his hand, came running in, and with him there came ten white horses with red plumes on their heads.

The ringmaster cracked his whip, and the horses cantered around the ring. Then he cracked his whip again, and they all

stood with their front legs up on the railing that circled the ring.
One of the horses had stopped just in front of the children. Annika
didn't like having a horse so close to her, so she crouched back in
her chair as far as she could. But Pippi leaned forward, lifted up
the horse's front leg, and said, "How's yourself? My horse sends his
regards to you. It's *his* birthday, too, today, though he has bows
on his tail instead of his head."

As luck would have it, Pippi let go of the horse's foot before
the ringmaster cracked his whip the next time, because then all the
horses jumped down from the railing and began to canter again.

When the act was finished, the ringmaster bowed beautifully,
and the horses trotted out. A second later, the curtain opened
again for a coal-black horse, and on his back stood a beautiful
lady dressed in green silk tights. Her name was Miss Carmencita,
it said in the program.

The horse trotted around in the sawdust, and Miss Carmencita
stood there calmly and smiled. But then something happened. Just
as the horse passed Pippi's place, something came whistling
through the air. It was none other than Pippi herself. There she
suddenly stood on the horse's back behind Miss Carmencita. At
first, Miss Carmencita was so astonished that she nearly fell off the
horse. Then she became angry. She began to hit behind herself
with her hands in order to get Pippi to jump off. But she couldn't
manage it.

"Calm down a little," said Pippi. "You're not the only one who's
going to have fun. There are others who've paid *their* money, too,
believe it or not!"

Then Miss Carmencita wanted to jump off herself, but she
couldn't do that either, for Pippi had a steady hold around her
waist. The people in the circus couldn't help laughing. It looked
so silly, they thought, to see the beautiful Miss Carmencita held

fast by a little redheaded scamp who stood on the horse's back in her big shoes looking as if she'd never done anything *but* perform in a circus.

But the ringmaster didn't laugh. He made a sign to his red-coated attendants to run forward and stop the horse.

"Is the act over already?" said Pippi, disappointed. "Just now when we were having such fun!"

"Derrible child," hissed the ringmaster between his teeth, "go away!"

Pippi looked sorrowfully at him. "Well, but, now," she said, "why are you so angry with me? I thought everyone was supposed to have a nice time here."

She jumped down from the horse, and went and sat down in her place. But now two big attendants came to throw her out. They took hold of her and tried to lift her.

It was no use. Pippi just sat still, and it simply wasn't possible to move her from the spot, though they tugged as hard as they could. So they shrugged their shoulders and went away.

In the meantime, the next act had begun. It was Miss Elvira, who was to walk the tightrope. She wore a pink tulle dress and carried a pink parasol in her hand. With small neat steps she ran out onto the rope. She swung her legs and did all manner of tricks. It was very pretty indeed. She proved, too, that she could go backwards on the thin rope. But when she came back to the little platform at the end of the line and turned around, Pippi was standing there.

"What was it you said?" said Pippi, delighted to see Miss Elvira's surprised expression.

Miss Elvira didn't say anything at all, but jumped down from the rope and threw her arms around the neck of the ringmaster, who was her father. Again he sent for his attendants to throw

Pippi out. This time he sent for five. But all the people in the circus shouted, "Let her be! We want to see the little redhead!"

And they stamped their feet and clapped their hands.

Pippi ran out on the line. And Miss Elvira's tricks were nothing compared to what Pippi could do. When she came to the middle of the rope, she stretched one leg straight up into the air, and her big shoe spread out like a roof over her head. She waggled her foot a little, to scratch behind her ear.

The ringmaster was not the least bit pleased that Pippi was performing in his circus. He wanted to be rid of her. So he sneaked forward and loosened the mechanism that held the line tight, and he was sure that Pippi would fall off.

But she didn't. She began to swing the rope instead. Back and forth swayed the line, faster and faster swung Pippi, and then—suddenly—she took a leap into the air and landed right on the ringmaster. He was so frightened that he began to run.

"This horse is even more fun," said Pippi. "But why haven't you any tassels in your hair?"

Now Pippi thought it was time to turn back to Tommy and Annika. She climbed off the ringmaster and went and sat down, and then the next act was about to begin. There was a moment's delay, because the ringmaster first had to go out and drink a glass of water and comb his hair. But after that he came in, bowed to the audience, and said, "Ladies and chantlemen! In ze next moment, you vill zee vun of ze vunders uff all time, ze zdrongest man in ze vorld, Mighty Adolf, who nobody has effer beaten yet. And here he is, ladies and chantlemen. Mighty Adolf!"

A gigantic man stepped into the ring. He was dressed in scarlet tights, and he had a leopardskin around his stomach. He bowed to the audience, and looked very self-satisfied indeed.

"Just *look* at which mossels!" said the ringmaster, squeezing

Mighty Adolf's arm where the muscles bulged like bowls under the skin.

"And now, ladies and chantlemen, I giff you a grrreat offer! Weech of you dares to try a wrestling match with Mighty Adolf, who dares to try to beat ze vorld's zdrongest man? A hundred crowns I pay to the vun who can beat Mighty Adolf. A hundred crowns, consider it, ladies and chantlemen! Step right up! Who'll giff it a try?"

Nobody came forward.

"What did he say?" asked Pippi. "And why is he speaking Arabian?"

"He said that the person who can beat that great big man over there will get a hundred crowns," said Tommy.

"I can do it," said Pippi. "But I think it would be a shame to beat him, 'cause he looks like such a nice man."

"But you could *never* do it," said Annika. "Why, that's the strongest man in the world!"

"Man, yes," said Pippi. "But I'm the strongest *girl* in the world, don't forget."

In the meantime, Mighty Adolf was lifting dumbbells and bending thick iron bars to show how strong he was.

"Now, now, goot people!" shouted the ringmaster. "Is there rilly nobody who should like to vin a hundred crowns? Must I rilly keep them for myself?" he said, waving a hundred-crown note.

"No, I rilly don't think you must," said Pippi, climbing over the railing to the ring.

"Go! Disappear! I don't vant I should zee you," the ringmaster hissed.

"Why are you always so unfriendly?" said Pippi reproachfully. "I only want to fight with Mighty Adolf."

"Zis is no time for chokes," said the ringmaster. "Go avay,

before Mighty Adolf hears your impertinence!"

But Pippi went right past the ringmaster and over to Mighty Adolf. She took his big hand in hers and shook it heartily.

"Now, shall we have a bit of a wrestle, you and I?" she said.

Mighty Adolf looked at her and didn't understand a thing.

"In one minute I'm going to begin," said Pippi.

And she did. She grappled properly with Mighty Adolf, and before anyone knew how it had happened, she'd laid him flat on the mat. Mighty Adolf scrambled up, quite red in the face.

"Hurrah for Pippi!" shouted Tommy and Annika. All the people at the circus heard this, and so they shouted, "Hurrah for Pippi!" too. The ringmaster sat on the railing and wrung his hands. He was angry. But Mighty Adolf was angrier still. Never in his life had anything so terrible happened to him. But now he would show this little red-haired girl what kind of a man Mighty Adolf was! He rushed forward and took a strong grip on her, but Pippi stood as fast as a rock.

"You can do better than that," she said to encourage him. Then she prised herself free from his grip and, in a second, Mighty Adolf was lying on the mat again. Pippi stood beside him and waited. She didn't have to wait long. With a bellow he raised himself and stormed at her again.

"Tiddlelipom and poddeliday," said Pippi.

All the people at the circus stamped their feet and threw their caps up in the air, and shouted, "Hurrah for Pippi!"

The third time Mighty Adolf rushed at her, Pippi lifted him high into the air and carried him on her upstretched arms around the ring. After that, she laid him on the mat and held him there.

"Now, my boy, I think we've had enough of this sort of game," she said. "It won't get any more fun than this, anyway."

"Pippi is the winner! Pippi is the winner!" shouted all the

people at the circus. Mighty Adolf slunk out as fast as he could. And the ringmaster had to go forward and present Pippi with the hundred-crown note, though he looked as if he would rather have eaten her up.

"Here you are, my young lady, here is your hundred crowns."

"That?" said Pippi scornfully. "What should I do with that piece of paper? You can have it to wrap fish in, if you want!"

Then she went back to her place.

"This is a long-lasting circus, this one," she said to Tommy and Annika. "Forty winks might not do any harm. But wake me up if there's anything else I need to help with."

So she lay back in her chair and went to sleep immediately. There she lay snoring while clowns and sword swallowers and snake people showed their tricks to Tommy and Annika and all the other people at the circus.

"Somehow, I think Pippi was best of all," whispered Tommy to Annika.

Introduction

Katy Carr has five younger brothers and sisters and since the death of their mother, she has helped their well-meaning yet perplexed aunt to take care of them. But they all run circles around poor Aunt Izzie: playing rough games, exploring—never still for a moment. Katy longs to set the others a good example, but her head is so full of plans and schemes and building castles in the air that all her good resolutions are quickly forgotten. When she gets into a fight at school and her rowdy game gets out of control, she vows never to get into a scrape again. But what does poor, thoughtless Katy do the following Monday? Well, having been cooped up inside all day because of the rain doesn't help her good intentions. . . .

WHAT KATY DID

SUSAN COOLIDGE

Kikeri

Katy was naturally fond of reading. Papa encouraged it. He kept a few books locked up, and then turned her loose in the library. She read all sorts of things: travels, and sermons, and old magazines. Nothing was so dull that she couldn't get through with it. Anything really interesting absorbed her so that she never knew what was going on about her. The little girls to whose houses she went visiting had found this out, and always hid away their storybooks when she was expected to tea. If they didn't do this, she was sure to pick one up and plunge in, and then it was no use to call her or tug at her dress, for she neither saw nor heard anything more till it was time to go home.

This afternoon she read the *Jerusalem* till it was too dark to see anymore. On her way upstairs she met Aunt Izzie, with bonnet and shawl on.

"Where *have* you been?" she said. "I have been calling you for the last half hour."

"I didn't hear you, ma'am."

"But where were you?" persisted Miss Izzie.

"In the library, reading," replied Katy.

Her aunt gave a sort of sniff, but she knew Katy's ways, and said no more.

"I'm going out to drink tea with Mrs. Hall and attend the evening lecture," she went on. "Be sure that Clover gets her lesson, and if Cecy comes over as usual, you must send her home early. All of you must be in bed by nine."

"Yes'm," said Katy; but I fear she was not attending much, but thinking in her secret soul, how jolly it was to have Aunt Izzie go out for once. Miss Carr was very faithful to her duties, and seldom left the children, even for an evening; so whenever she did, they felt a certain sense of novelty and freedom, which was dangerous as well as pleasant.

Still, I am sure that on this occasion Katy meant no mischief. Like all excitable people, she seldom did *mean* to do wrong; she just did it when it came into her head. Supper passed off successfully, and all might have gone well had it not been that after the lessons were learned and Cecy had come in, they fell to talking about "Kikeri."

Kikeri was a game which had been very popular with them a year before. They had invented it themselves, and chosen for it this queer name out of an old fairy story. It was a sort of mixture of Blindman's Bluff and Tag—only, instead of anyone's eyes being bandaged, they all played in the dark. One of the children would stay out in the hall, which was dimly lighted from the stairs, while the others hid themselves in the nursery. When they were all hidden they would call out "Kikeri!" as a signal for the one in the hall to come in and find them. Of course, coming from the light he could see nothing, while the others could see only dimly. It was very exciting to stand crouching up in a corner and watch the dark figure stumbling about and feeling to right and left, while every now and then somebody, just escaping his clutches, would slip past and gain the hall—which was "Freedom Castle"—with a joyful shout of "Kikeri, Kikeri, Kikeri, Ki!" Whoever was caught had to take the place of the catcher. For a long time this game was the delight of the Carr children; but so many scratches and black-and-blue spots came of it, and so many of the nursery things were thrown down and broken, that at last Aunt Izzie issued an order that it should not be played anymore. This was almost a year since; but talking of it now put it into their heads to want to try it again.

"After all, we didn't promise," said Cecy.

"No, and *Papa* never said a word about our not playing it," added Katy, to whom "Papa" was authority, and must always be minded, while Aunt Izzie might now and then be defied.

So they all went upstairs. Dorry and John, though half undressed, were allowed to join the game. Philly was fast asleep in another room.

It was certainly splendid fun. Once Clover climbed up on the mantelpiece and sat there, and when Katy, who was finder, groped about a little more wildly than usual, she caught hold of Clover's foot, and couldn't imagine where it came from. Dorry got a hard knock, and cried, and at another time Katy's dress caught on the bureau handle and was frightfully torn; but these were too much affairs of every day to interfere in the least with the pleasures of Kikeri. The fun and frolic seemed to grow greater the longer they

played. In the excitement, time went on so much faster than any
of them dreamed. Suddenly, in the midst of the noise, came a
sound—the sharp distinct slam of the carryall door at the side
entrance. Aunt Izzie had returned from her lecture!

The dismay and confusion of that moment! Cecy slipped
downstairs like an eel, and fled on the wings of fear along the
path which led to her home. Mrs. Hall, as she bade Aunt Izzie
good night, and shut Dr. Carr's front door behind her with a bang,
might have been struck with the singular fact that a distant bang
came from her own front door like a sort of echo. But she was not
a suspicious woman; and when she went upstairs there were
Cecy's clothes neatly folded on a chair, and Cecy herself in bed,
fast asleep, only with a little more color than usual in her cheeks.

Meantime, Aunt Izzie was on *her* way upstairs and such a panic
as prevailed in the nursery! Katy felt it, and basely scuttled off to
her own room, where she went to bed with all possible speed. But
the others found it much harder to go to bed; there were so many
of them, all getting into each other's way, and with no lamp to see
by. Dorry and John popped under the clothes half undressed, Elsie
disappeared, and Clover, too late for either, and hearing Aunt
Izzie's step in the hall, did this horrible thing—fell on her knees
with her face buried in a chair, and began to say her prayers very
hard indeed.

Aunt Izzie, coming in with a candle in her hand, stood in the
doorway, astonished at the spectacle. She sat down and waited for
Clover to get through, while Clover, on her part, didn't dare to get
through, but went on repeating "Now I lay me" over and over
again, in a sort of despair. At last Aunt Izzie said very grimly: "That
will do, Clover, you can get up!" and Clover rose, feeling like a
culprit, which she was, for it was much naughtier to pretend to
be praying than to disobey Aunt Izzie and be out of bed after

ten o'clock, though I think Clover hardly understood this then.

Aunt Izzie began at once to undress her, and while doing so asked so many questions, and before long she had got at the truth of the whole matter. She gave Clover a sharp scolding; and, leaving her to wash her tearful face, she went to the bed where John and Dorry lay fast asleep and snoring as conspicuously as they knew how. Something strange in the appearance of the bed made her look more closely; she lifted the clothes, and there, sure enough, they were—half dressed, and with their school boots on.

Such a shake as Aunt Izzie gave the little scamps at this discovery would have roused a couple of dormice. Much against their will, John and Dorry were forced to wake up and be slapped and scolded, and made ready for bed, Aunt Izzie standing over them all the while, like a dragon. She had just tucked them warmly in, when for the first time she missed Elsie.

"Where is my poor Elsie?" she exclaimed.

"In bed," said Clover, meekly.

"In bed!" repeated Aunt Izzie, much amazed. Then stooping down she gave a vigorous pull. The trundle bed came into view, and, sure enough, there was Elsie, in full dress, shoes and all, but so fast asleep that not all Aunt Izzie's shakes and pinches and calls were able to rouse her. Her clothes were taken off, her boots unlaced, her nightgown put on; but through it all, Elsie slept, and she was the only one of the children who did not get the scolding she deserved that dreadful night.

Katy did not even pretend to be asleep when Aunt Izzie went to her room. Her tardy conscience had woken up, and she was lying in bed, very miserable at having drawn the others into a scrape as well as herself, and at the failure of her last set of resolutions about "setting an example to the younger ones." So unhappy was she, that Aunt Izzie's severe words were almost a relief; and though she cried herself to sleep, it was rather from the burden of her own thoughts than because she had been scolded.

She cried even harder the next day, for Dr. Carr talked to her more seriously than he had ever done before. He reminded her of the time when her Mamma died, and of how she said, "Katy must be a Mamma to the little ones, when she grows up." And he asked her if she didn't think the time was come for beginning to take this dear place toward the children. Poor Katy! She sobbed as if her heart would break at this, and though she made no promises, I think she was never so thoughtless again after that day.

As for the rest, Papa called them together and made them distinctly understand that "Kikeri" was never to be played anymore. It was so seldom that Papa forbade any games, however boisterous, that this order really made an impression on the unruly brood, and they never have played Kikeri again from that day to this.

Introduction

It all begins on a hot summer afternoon when the White Rabbit runs past Alice as she lies dozing in a meadow, takes a watch out of his waistcoat pocket, and hurries down a large rabbit hole. Not once considering how she will get out, Alice follows him— down, down, into a topsy-turvy world where anything can happen. She shrinks to just ten inches tall one minute, the next she grows to a massive nine feet. Remarkable characters appear at every turn, and Alice has the strangest adventures. She swims with a mouse, takes advice from a caterpillar smoking a hookah, chats to the grinning Cheshire Cat, cradles a baby who turns into a pig, and argues with two fishy liveried footmen. Nothing is what it seems in Wonderland, and when Alice reaches the March Hare's house, there is something even more curious in store for her.

ALICE'S ADVENTURES IN WONDERLAND

LEWIS CARROLL

A Mad Tea Party

There was a table set out under a tree in front of the house, and the March Hare and the Hatter were having tea at it: a Dormouse was sitting between them, fast asleep, and the other two were using it as a cushion, resting their elbows on it, and talking over its head. "Very uncomfortable for the Dormouse," thought Alice; "only, as it's asleep, I suppose it doesn't mind."

The table was a large one, but the three were all crowded together at one corner of it. "No room! No room!" they cried out when they saw Alice coming. "There's *plenty* of room!" said Alice indignantly, and she sat down in a large armchair at one end of the table.

"Have some wine," the March Hare said in an encouraging tone.

Alice looked all around the table, but there was nothing on it but tea. "I don't see any wine," she remarked.

"There isn't any," said the March Hare.

"Then it wasn't very civil of you to offer it," said Alice angrily.

"It wasn't very civil of you to sit down without being invited," said the March Hare.

"I didn't know it was *your* table," said Alice; "it's laid for a great many more than three."

"Your hair wants cutting," said the Hatter. He had been looking at Alice for some time with great curiosity, and this was his first speech.

"You should learn not to make personal remarks," Alice said with some severity, "it's very rude."

The Hatter opened his eyes very wide on hearing this; but all he *said* was, "Why is a raven like a writing desk?"

"Come, we shall have some fun now!" thought Alice. "I'm glad they've begun asking riddles.—I believe I can guess that," she added aloud.

"Do you mean that you think you can find out the answer to it?" said the March Hare.

"Exactly so," said Alice.

"Then you should say what you mean," the March Hare went on.

"I do," Alice hastily replied, "at least—at least I mean what I say—that's the same thing, you know."

"Not the same thing a bit!" said the Hatter. "You might just as well say that 'I see what I eat' is the same thing as 'I eat what I see'!"

"You might just as well say," added the March Hare, "that 'I like what I get' is the same thing as 'I get what I like'!"

"You might just as well say," added the Dormouse, who seemed to be talking in his sleep, "that 'I breathe when I sleep' is the same thing as 'I sleep when I breathe'!"

"It *is* the same thing with you," said the Hatter, and here the conversation dropped, and the party sat silent for a minute, while Alice thought over all she could remember about ravens and writing desks, which wasn't much.

The Hatter was the first to break the silence.

"What day of the month is it?" he said, turning to Alice; he had taken his watch out of his pocket, and was looking at it uneasily, shaking it every now and then, and holding it to his ear.

Alice considered a little, and then said, "The fourth."

"Two days wrong!" sighed the Hatter. "I told you butter wouldn't suit the works!" he added, looking angrily at the March Hare.

"It was the *best* butter," the March Hare meekly replied.

"Yes, but some crumbs must have got in as well," the Hatter grumbled: "you shouldn't have put it in with the bread knife."

The March Hare took the watch and looked at it gloomily: then he dipped it into his cup of tea, and looked at it again: but he could think of nothing better to say than his first remark, "It was the *best* butter, you know."

Alice had been looking over his shoulder with some curiosity. "What a funny watch!" she remarked. "It tells the day of the month, and doesn't tell what o'clock it is!"

"Why should it?" muttered the Hatter. "Does *your* watch tell you what year it is?"

"Of course not," Alice replied very readily, "but that's because it stays the same year for such a long time together."

"Which is just the case with *mine*," said the Hatter.

Alice felt dreadfully puzzled. The Hatter's remark seemed to have no sort of meaning in it, and yet it was certainly English. "I don't quite understand you," she said, as politely as she could.

"The Dormouse is asleep again," said the Hatter, and he poured a little hot tea upon its nose.

The Dormouse shook its head impatiently, and said, without opening its eyes, "Of course, of course; just what I was going to remark myself."

"Have you guessed the riddle yet?" the Hatter said, turning to Alice again.

"No, I give it up," Alice replied, "what's the answer?"

"I haven't the slightest idea," said the Hatter.

"Nor I," said the March Hare.

Alice sighed wearily. "I think you might do something better with the time," she said, "than wasting it in asking riddles that have no answers."

"If you knew Time as well as I do," said the Hatter, "you wouldn't talk about wasting *it*. It's *him*."

"I don't know what you mean," said Alice.

"Of course you don't!" the Hatter said, tossing his head contemptuously. "I dare say you never even spoke to Time!"

"Perhaps not," Alice cautiously replied, "but I know I have to beat time when I learn music."

"Ah! that accounts for it," said the Hatter. "He won't stand beating. Now, if you only kept on good terms with him, he'd do almost anything you liked with the clock. For instance, suppose it were nine o'clock in the morning, just time to begin lessons: you'd only have to whisper a hint to Time, and around goes the clock in a twinkling! Half past one, time for dinner!"

("I only wish it was," the March Hare said to itself in a whisper.)

"That would be grand, certainly," said Alice thoughtfully, "but then—I shouldn't be hungry for it, you know."

"Not at first, perhaps," said the Hatter, "but you could keep it to half past one as long as you liked."

"Is that the way *you* manage?" Alice asked.

The Hatter shook his head mournfully. "Not I!" he replied. "We quarreled last March—just before *he* went mad, you know—" (pointing with his teaspoon at the March Hare) "—it was at the great concert given by the Queen of Hearts, and I had to sing:

> *'Twinkle, twinkle, little bat!*
> *How I wonder what you're at!'*

You know the song, perhaps?"

"I've heard something like it," said Alice.

"It goes on, you know," the Hatter continued, "in this way:

> *'Up above the world you fly,*
> *Like a tea tray in the sky.*
> *Twinkle, twinkle—'"*

Here the Dormouse shook itself, and began singing in its sleep,

"Twinkle, twinkle, twinkle, twinkle—" and went on so long that they had to pinch it to make it stop.

"Well, I'd hardly finished the first verse," said the Hatter, "when the Queen jumped up and bawled out, 'He's murdering the time! Off with his head!'"

"How dreadfully savage!" exclaimed Alice.

"And ever since that," the Hatter went on in a mournful tone, "he won't do a thing I ask! It's always six o'clock now."

A bright idea came into Alice's head. "Is that the reason so many tea things are put out here?" she asked.

"Yes, that's it," said the Hatter with a sigh, "it's always teatime, and we've no time to wash the things between whiles."

"Then you keep moving around, I suppose?" said Alice.

"Exactly so," said the Hatter, "as the things get used up."

"But what happens when you come to the beginning again?" Alice ventured to ask.

"Suppose we change the subject," the March Hare interrupted, yawning. "I'm getting tired of this. I vote the young lady tells us a story."

"I'm afraid I don't know one," said Alice, rather alarmed at the proposal.

"Then the Dormouse shall!" they both cried. "Wake up, Dormouse!" And they pinched it on both sides at once.

The Dormouse slowly opened his eyes. "I wasn't asleep," he said in a hoarse, feeble voice, "I heard every word you fellows were saying."

"Tell us a story!" said the March Hare.

"Yes, please do!" pleaded Alice.

"And be quick about it," added the Hatter, "or you'll be asleep again before it's done."

"Once upon a time there were three little sisters," the

Dormouse began in a great hurry, "and their names were Elsie, Lacie, and Tillie; and they lived at the bottom of a well—"

"What did they live on?" said Alice, who always took a great interest in questions of eating and drinking.

"They lived on treacle," said the Dormouse, after thinking a minute or two.

"They couldn't have done that, you know," Alice gently remarked, "they'd have been ill."

"So they were," said the Dormouse, "*very* ill."

Alice tried to fancy to herself what such an extraordinary way of living would be like, but it puzzled her too much, so she went on: "But why did they live at the bottom of a well?"

"Take some more tea," the March Hare said to Alice, very earnestly.

"I've had nothing yet," Alice replied in an offended tone, "so I can't take more."

"You mean you can't take *less*," said the Hatter, "it's very easy to take *more* than nothing."

"Nobody asked *your* opinion," said Alice.

"Who's making personal remarks now?" the Hatter asked triumphantly.

Alice did not quite know what to say to this, so she helped herself to some tea and bread and butter, and then turned to the Dormouse, and repeated her question. "Why did they live at the bottom of a well?"

The Dormouse again took a minute or two to think about it, and then said, "It was a treacle well."

"There's no such thing!" Alice was beginning very angrily, but the Hatter and the March Hare went "Sh! Sh!" and the Dormouse sulkily remarked, "If you can't be civil, you'd better finish the story for yourself."

"No, please go on!" Alice said very humbly, "I won't interrupt again. I dare say there may be *one*."

"One, indeed!" said the Dormouse indignantly. However, he consented to go on. "And so these three little sisters—they were learning to draw, you know—"

"What did they draw?" said Alice, quite forgetting her promise.

"Treacle," said the Dormouse, without considering at all this time.

"I want a clean cup," interrupted the Hatter, "let's all move one place on."

He moved on as he spoke, and the Dormouse followed him: the March Hare moved into the Dormouse's place, and Alice rather unwillingly took the place of the March Hare. The Hatter was the only one who got any advantage from the change: and Alice was a good deal worse off than before, as the March Hare had just upset the milk jug into his plate.

Alice did not wish to offend the Dormouse again, so she began very cautiously: "But I don't understand. Where did they draw the treacle from?"

"You can draw water out of a water well," said the Hatter, "so I should think you could draw treacle out of a treacle well—eh, stupid?"

"But they were *in* the well," Alice said to the Dormouse, not choosing to notice this last remark.

"Of course they were," said the Dormouse, "—well in."

This answer so confused poor Alice, that she let the Dormouse go on for some time without interrupting it.

"They were learning to draw," the Dormouse went on, yawning and rubbing its eyes, for it was getting very sleepy, "and they drew all manner of things—everything that begins with an M—"

"Why with an M?" said Alice.

"Why not?" said the March Hare.

Alice was silent.

The Dormouse had closed its eyes by this time, and was going off into a doze; but, on being pinched by the Hatter, it woke up again with a little shriek, and went on: "—that begins with an M, such as mousetraps, and the moon, and memory, and muchness—you know you say things are 'much of a muchness'—did you ever see such a thing as a drawing of a muchness?"

"Really, now you ask me," said Alice, very much confused, "I don't think—"

"Then you shouldn't talk," said the Hatter.

This piece of rudeness was more than Alice could bear: she got up in great disgust, and walked off; the Dormouse fell asleep instantly, and neither of the others took the least notice of her going, though she looked back once or twice, half hoping that they would call after her; the last time she saw them, they were trying to put the Dormouse into the teapot.

"At any rate, I'll never go *there* again!" said Alice as she picked her way through the wood. "It's the stupidest tea party I ever was at in all my life!"

*"Without doubt Judy was the worst of the seven,
probably because she was the cleverest." So Ethel
Turner describes the most highly spirited member
of Captain Woolcot's large family, who all run wild
in their rambling riverside home in Sydney. The
Captain calls them "a disgraceful tribe" and after a
particularly naughty episode, forbids them to go to
the pantomime they are so looking forward to. The
next day, Pat, the stable lad, is taking the dogcart
into town for repairs. Pip, the eldest boy, goes with
him, to deliver a coat to his father ("the governor")
at the army barracks. Judy (christened Helen and
sometimes called Fizz) goes along for the ride,
taking with her the youngest member of the family,
the baby they call "the General."*

Seven Little Australians

Ethel Turner

The General Sees Active Service

On the way to Paddington a gentleman on horseback slackened pace a little. Pip took off his hat with a flourish, and Judy gave a frank, pleased smile, for it was a certain old Colonel they had known for years, and had cause to remember his good humor and liberality.

"Well, my little maid—well, Philip, lad," he said smiling genially, while his horse danced around the dogcart, "And the General too— where are you all off to?"

"The Barracks. I'm taking something up for the governor," Pip answered. Judy was watching the plunging horse with admiring eyes. "And then we're going back home."

The old gentleman managed, in spite of the horse's tricks, to slip his hand in his pocket. "Here's something to make yourself ill with on the way," he said, handing them two half-crowns, "but don't send me the doctor's bill."

He flicked the General's cheek with his whip, gave Judy a nod, and cantered off.

The children looked at each other with sparkling eyes.

"Coconuts," Pip said, "and tarts and toffee, and save the rest for a football?" Judy shook her head.

"Where do *I* come in?" she said. "You'd keep the football at school. I vote pink jujubes, and ice creams, and a wax doll."

"A wax grandmother!" Pip retorted. "You wouldn't be such a girl, I hope." Then he added, with almost pious fervor, "Thank goodness you've always hated dolls, Fizz."

Judy gave a sudden leap in her seat, almost upsetting the General, and bringing down upon her head a storm of reproaches from the coachman. "*I* know!" she said. "And we're almost halfway there now. Oh-h-h! it *will* be lovely."

Pip urged her to explain herself.

"Bondi Aquarium—skating, boats, merry-go-round, switchback threepence a go!" she returned succinctly.

"Good iron," Pip whistled softly, while he revolved the thing in his mind. "There'd be something over, too, to get some tucker with, and perhaps something for the football, too." Then his brow clouded.

"There's the kid—whatever did you go bringing him for? Just like a girl to spoil everything!"

Judy looked nonplussed. "I quite forgot him," she said, vexedly. "Couldn't we leave him somewhere? Couldn't we ask someone to take care of him while we go? Oh, it would be *too* bad to have to give it up just because of him. It's beginning to rain, too. We couldn't take him with us."

They were at the foot of Barrack Hill now, and Pat told them they must get out and walk the rest of the way up, or he would never get the dogcart finished to take back that evening.

Pip tumbled out and took the General, all in a bunched-up heap,

and Judy alighted carefully after him, the precious coat parcel in her arms. And they walked up the asphalt hill to the gate leading to the officers' quarters in utter silence.

"Well?" Pip said querulously, as they reached the top. "Be quick—haven't you thought of anything?"

That leveling of brows, and pursing of lips, always meant deep and intricate calculation on his sister's part, as he knew full well.

"Yes," Judy said quietly. "I've got a plan that will do, I think." Then a sudden fire entered her manner.

"Who is the General's father? Tell me that," she said, in a rapid, eager way. "And isn't it right and proper fathers should look after their sons? And doesn't he deserve we should get even with him for doing us out of the pantomime? And isn't the Aquarium too lovely to miss?"

"Well?" Pip said. His slower brain did not follow such rapid reasoning.

"Only I'm going to leave the General here at the Barracks for a couple of hours till we come back, his father being the proper person to watch over him." Judy grasped the General's small fat hand in a determined way, and opened the gate.

"Oh, I say," remarked Pip, "we'll get into an awful row, you know, Fizz. I don't think we'd better—I don't really know, old girl."

"Not a bit," said Judy stoutly, "at least, only a bit, and the Aquarium's worth that. Look how it's raining—the child will get croup, or rheumatism, or something if we take him. There's Father standing over on the green near the tennis court talking to a man. I'll slip quietly along the veranda and into his own room, and put the coat and the General on the bed; then I'll tell a soldier to go and tell Father his parcels have come, and while he's gone I'll fly back to you, and we'll catch the tram and go to the Aquarium."

Pip whistled again, softly. He was used to bold proposals from this sister of his, but this was beyond everything. "B-b-but," he said uneasily, "but, Judy, whatever would he do with that kid for two mortal hours?"

"Mind him," Judy returned promptly. "It's a pretty thing if a father can't mind his own child for two hours. Afterward, you see, when we've been to the Aquarium, we will come back and fetch him, and we can explain to Father how it was raining and that we thought we'd better not take him with us for fear of rheumatism, and that we were in a hurry to catch the tram, and as he wasn't in his room we just put him on the bed till he came. Why, Pip, it's beautifully simple!"

Pip still looked uncomfortable. "I don't like it, Fizz," he said again. "He'll be in a fearful wax."

Judy gave him one exasperated look. "Go and see if that's the Bondi tram coming," she said, and, glad of a moment's respite, he went down the path again to the pavement and looked down the hill. When he turned around again she had gone.

He stuck his hands in his pockets and walked up and down the path a few times. "Fizz'll get us hanged yet," he muttered, looking darkly at the door in the wall through which she had disappeared.

He pushed his hat to the back of his head and stared gloomily at his boots, wondering what would be the consequences of this new mischief. There was a light footfall behind him.

"Come on," said Judy, pulling his sleeve, "it's done now, come on, let's go and have our fun. Have you got the money safe?"

It was two o'clock as they passed out of the gate and turned their faces up the hill to the tram stopping-place. And it was half past four when they jumped out of a town-bound tram and entered the gates again to pick up their charge.

Such an afternoon as they had had! Once inside the Aquarium, even Pip had put his conscience qualms on one side, and bent all his energies to enjoying himself thoroughly. And Judy was like a

little mad thing. She spent a shilling of her money on the switchback
railway, pronouncing the swift, bewildering motion "heavenly." The
first journey made Pip feel sick, so he eschewed a repetition of it, and
watched Judy go off from time to time, waving gaily from the perilous
little car, almost with his heart in his mouth. Then they hired a pair
of roller skates each, and bruised themselves black and blue with
heavy falls on the asphalt. After that they had a ride on the merry-
go-round, but Judy found it tame after the switchback, and refused
to squander a second threepence on it, contenting herself with
watching Pip fly around, and madly running by his side to keep up
as long as she could. They finished the afternoon with a prolonged
inspection of the fish tanks, a light repast of jam tarts of
questionable freshness, and twopenny-worth of peanuts. And, as I
said, it was half past four as they hastened up the path again to the
top gate of the Barracks.

"I *hope* he's been good," Judy said, as she turned the handle.
"Yes, you come, too, Pip,"—for that young gentleman hung back
one agonized second—"twenty kicks or blows divided by two only
make ten, you see."

They went up the long stone veranda and stopped at one door.
There was a little knot of young officers laughing and talking close by.

"Take my word, 'twas as good as a play to see Wooly grabbing
his youngster, and stuffing it into a cab, and getting in himself, all
with a look of ponderous injured dignity," one said, and laughed
at the recollection.

Another blew away a cloud of cigar smoke. "It was a jolly little
beggar," he said. "It doubled its fists and landed His High Mightiness
one in the eye—and then its shoe dropped off, and we all rushed
to pick it up, and it was muddy and generally dilapidated, and old
Wooly went red slowly up to his ear-tips as he tried to put it on."

A little figure stepped into the middle of the group—a little figure with an impossibly short and shabby ulster, thin, black-stockinged, legs, and a big hat crushed over a tangle of curls.

"It is my father you are speaking of," she said, her head very high, her tone haughty, "and I cannot tell where your amusement is. Is my father here, or did I hear you say he had gone away?"

Two of the men looked foolish, the third took off his cap.

"I am sorry you should have overheard us, Miss Woolcot," he said pleasantly. "Still, there is no irreparable harm done, is there? Yes, your father has gone away in a cab. He couldn't imagine how the little boy came on his bed, and, as he couldn't keep him here very well, I suppose he has taken him home."

Something like a look of shame came into Judy's bright eyes.

"I am afraid I must have put my father to some inconvenience," she said quietly. "It was I who left the Gen—my brother here, because I didn't know what to do with him for an hour or two. But I quite meant to take him home myself. Has he been gone long?"

"About half an hour," the officer said, and tried not to look amused at the little girl's old-fashioned manner.

"Ah, thank you. Perhaps we can catch him up. Come on, Pip," and, nodding in a grave, distant manner, she turned away, and went down the veranda and through the gate with her brother.

"A nice hole we're in," he said.

Judy nodded.

"It's about the very awfulest thing we've ever done in our lives. Fancy the governor carting that child all the way from here! Oh, lor'!"

Judy nodded again.

"Can't you speak?" he said irritably. "You've got us into this—I didn't want to do it—but I'll stand by you, of course. Only you'll have to think of something quick."

Judy bit three fingertips off her right-hand glove, and looked melancholy.

"There's absolutely nothing to do, Pip," she said slowly. "I didn't think it would turn out like this. I suppose we'd better just go straight back and hand ourselves over for punishment. He'll be too angry to hear any sort of an excuse, so we'd better just grin and bear whatever he does to us. I'm really sorry, too, that I made a laughingstock of him up there."

Pip was explosive. He called her a little ass and a gowk and a stupid idiot for doing such a thing, and she did not reproach him or answer back once.

They caught a tram and went into Sydney, and afterward to the boat. They ensconced themselves in a corner at the far end, and discussed the state of affairs with much seriousness. Then Pip got up and strolled about a little to relieve his feelings, coming back in a second with a white, scared face.

"He's on the boat," he said, in a horrified whisper.

"Where—where—where? What—what—what?" Judy cried, unintentionally mimicking a long-buried monarch.

"In the cabin, looking as glum as a boiled wallaby, and hanging on to the poor little General as if he thinks he'll fly away."

Judy looked a little frightened for the first time.

"Can't we hide? Don't let him see us. It wouldn't be any good offering to take the General now. We're in for it now, Pip—there'll be no quarter."

Pip groaned, then Judy stood up.

"Let's creep down as far as the engine," she said, "and see if he does look very bad."

They made their way cautiously along the deck, and took up a position where they could see without being seen. The dear little General was sitting on the seat next to his stern father, who had a firm hold of the back of his woolly pelisse. He was sucking his little dirty hand, and casting occasional longing glances at his tan shoe, which he knew was delicious to bite. Once or twice he had pulled it off and conveyed it to his mouth, but his father intercepted it, and angrily buttoned it on again in its rightful place. He wanted, too, to slither off that horrid seat, and crawl all over the deck, and explore the ground under the seats, and see where the puffing noise came from, but there was that iron grasp on his coat that no amount of wriggling would move. No wonder the poor child looked unhappy.

At last the boat stopped at a wharf not far from Misrule, and the Captain alighted, carrying his small dirty son gingerly in his arms. He walked slowly up the red road along which the dogcart had sped so blithesomely some six or seven hours ago, and Judy and Pip followed at a respectful—a very respectful—distance. At the gate he saw them, and gave a large, angry beckon for them to come up. Judy went very white, but obeyed instantly, and Pip, pulling himself together, brought up the rear.

Afterward Judy only had a very indistinct remembrance of what happened during the next half hour. She knew there was a stormy scene, in which Esther and the whole family came in for an immense amount of vituperation.

Then Pip received a thrashing, in spite of Judy's persistent avowal that it was all her fault, and Pip hadn't done anything. She remembered wondering whether she would be treated as summarily as Pip, so angry was her father's face as he pushed the boy aside and stood looking at her, riding whip in hand.

But he flung it down and laid a heavy hand on her shrinking shoulder.

"Next Monday," he said slowly—"next Monday morning you will be going to boarding school. Esther, kindly see Helen's clothes are ready for boarding school—next Monday morning."

When Matthew Cuthbert goes to the station to pick up a boy from the orphanage to help on the farm, imagine his surprise to find that the "boy" is an eleven-year-old redheaded girl named Anne. He takes her back to the house with green gables, where his sister Marilla is most displeased to be offered this odd girl as a helper. But her feistiness and impulsive nature intrigue Marilla, who soon invites Anne to make Green Gables her home. Life is full of things to do and places to explore. Best of all will be the Sunday school picnic beside the Lake of Shining Waters (as Anne has romantically renamed the local pond). Anne's imagination is filled with thoughts of boating on the lake with her new friend Diana—and of tasting ice cream for the first time. But will her dreams come true?

ANNE OF GREEN GABLES

L. M. MONTGOMERY

Anne's Confession

On the Monday evening before the picnic, Marilla came down from her room with a troubled face.

"Anne," she said to that small personage, who was shelling peas by the spotless table and singing "Nelly of the Hazel Dell" with a vigor and expression that did credit to Diana's teaching, "did you see anything of my amethyst brooch? I thought I stuck it in my pincushion when I came home from church yesterday evening, but I can't find it anywhere."

"I—I saw it this afternoon when you were away at the Aid Society," said Anne, a little slowly. "I was passing your door when I saw it on the cushion, so I went in to look at it."

"Did you touch it?" said Marilla sternly.

"Y-e-e-s," admitted Anne. "I took it up and I pinned it on my breast just to see how it would look."

"You had no business to do anything of the sort. It's very wrong in a little girl to meddle. You shouldn't have gone into my room in the first place and you shouldn't have touched a brooch that didn't belong to you in the second. Where did you put it?"

"Oh, I put it back on the bureau. I hadn't it on a minute. Truly, I didn't mean to meddle, Marilla. I didn't think about its being wrong to go in and try on the brooch; but I see now that it was, and I'll never do it again. That's one good thing about me. I never do the same naughty thing twice."

"You didn't put it back," said Marilla. "That brooch isn't anywhere on the bureau. You've taken it out or something, Anne."

"I *did* put it back," said Anne quickly—pertly, Marilla thought. "I just don't remember whether I stuck it on the pincushion or laid it in the china tray. But I'm perfectly certain I put it back."

"I'll go and have another look," said Marilla, determining to be just. "If you put that brooch back, it's there still. If it isn't, I'll know you didn't, that's all!"

Marilla went to her room and made a thorough search, not only over the bureau, but in every other place she thought the brooch might possibly be. It was not to be found and she returned to the kitchen.

"Anne, the brooch is gone. By your own admission you were the last person to handle it. Now, what have you done with it? Tell me the truth at once. Did you take it out and lose it?"

"No, I didn't," said Anne solemnly, meeting Marilla's angry gaze squarely. "I never took the brooch out of your room and that is the truth, if I was to be led to the block for it—although I'm not very certain what a block is. So there, Marilla."

Anne's "so there" was only intended to emphasize her

assertion, but Marilla took it as a display of defiance.

"I believe you are telling me a falsehood, Anne," she said sharply. "I know you are. There, now, don't say anything more unless you are prepared to tell the whole truth. Go to your room and stay there until you are ready to confess."

"Will I take the peas with me?" said Anne meekly.

"No, I'll finish shelling them myself. Do as I bid you."

When Anne was gone, Marilla went about her evening tasks in a very disturbed state of mind. She was worried about her valuable brooch. What if Anne had lost it? And how wicked of the child to deny having taken it, when anybody could see she must have! With such an innocent face, too!

"I don't know what I wouldn't sooner have had happen," thought Marilla, as she nervously shelled the peas. "Of course I don't suppose she meant to steal it or anything like that. She's just taken it to play with or help along that imagination of hers. She must have taken it, that's clear, for there hasn't been a soul in that room since she was in it, by her own story, until I went up tonight. And the brooch is gone, there's nothing surer. I suppose she has lost it and is afraid to own up for fear she'll be punished. It's a dreadful thing to think she tells falsehoods. It's a far worse thing than her fit of temper. It's a fearful responsibility to have a child in your house you can't trust. Slyness and untruthfulness—that's what she has displayed. I declare I feel worse about that than about the brooch. If she'd only have told the truth about it I wouldn't mind so much."

Marilla went to her room at intervals all through the evening and searched for the brooch, without finding it. A bedtime visit to the east gable produced no result. Anne persisted in denying that she knew anything about the brooch, but Marilla was only the more firmly convinced that she did.

She told Matthew the story the next morning. Matthew was confounded and puzzled; he could not so quickly lose faith in Anne, but he had to admit that circumstances were against her.

"You're sure it hasn't fell down behind the bureau?" was the only suggestion he could offer.

"I've moved the bureau and I've taken out the drawers and I've looked in every crack and cranny," was Marilla's positive answer. "The brooch is gone and that child has taken it and lied about it. That's the plain, ugly truth, Matthew Cuthbert, and we might as well look it in the face."

"Well, now, what are you going to do about it?" Matthew asked forlornly, feeling secretly thankful that Marilla and not he had to deal with the situation. He felt no desire to put his oar in this time.

"She'll stay in her room until she confesses," said Marilla grimly, remembering the success of this method in the former case. "Then we'll see. Perhaps we'll be able to find the brooch if she'll only tell where she took it; but in any case she'll have to be severely punished, Matthew."

"Well, now, you'll have to punish her," said Matthew, reaching for his hat. "I've nothing to do with it, remember. You warned me off yourself."

Marilla felt deserted by everyone. She could not even go to Mrs. Lynde for advice. She went up to the east gable with a very serious face and left it with a face more serious still. Anne steadfastly refused to confess. She persisted in asserting that she had not taken the brooch. The child had evidently been crying and Marilla felt a pang of pity, which she sternly repressed. By night she was, as she expressed it, "beat out."

"You'll stay in this room until you confess, Anne. You can make up your mind to that," she said firmly.

"But the picnic is tomorrow, Marilla," cried Anne. "You won't keep me from going to that, will you? You'll just let me out for the afternoon, won't you? Then I'll stay here as long as you like afterward *cheerfully*. But I *must* go to the picnic."

"You'll not go to picnics nor anywhere else until you've confessed, Anne."

"Oh, Marilla," gasped Anne.

But Marilla had gone out and shut the door.

Wednesday morning dawned as bright and fair as if expressly made to order for the picnic. Birds sang around Green Gables; the Madonna lilies in the garden sent out whiffs of perfume that entered in on viewless winds at every door and window, and wandered through halls and rooms like spirits of benediction. The birches in the hollow waved joyful hands as if watching for Anne's usual morning greeting from the east gable. But Anne was not at her window. When Marilla took her breakfast up to her she found the child sitting primly on her bed, pale and resolute, with tight-shut lips and gleaming eyes.

"Marilla, I'm ready to confess."

"Ah!" Marilla laid down her tray. Once again her method had succeeded; but her success was very bitter to her. "Let me hear what you have to say then, Anne."

"I took the amethyst brooch," said Anne, as if repeating a lesson she had learned. "I took it just as you said. I didn't mean to take it when I went in. But it did look so beautiful, Marilla, when I pinned it on my breast that I was overcome by an irresistible temptation. I imagined how perfectly thrilling it would be to take it to Idlewild and play I was the Lady Cordelia Fitzgerald. It would be so much easier to imagine I was the Lady Cordelia if I had a real amethyst brooch on. Diana and I made necklaces of roseberries, but what are roseberries compared to amethysts? So I took the brooch. I thought I could put it back before you came home. I went all the way around by the road to lengthen out the time. When I was going over the bridge across the Lake of Shining Waters I took the brooch off to have another look at it. Oh, how it did shine in the sunlight! And then, when I was leaning over the bridge, it just slipped through my fingers—so—and went down—down—down, all purply-sparkling and sank for evermore beneath the Lake of Shining Waters. And that's the best I can do at confessing, Marilla."

Marilla felt hot anger surge up into her heart again. This child had taken and lost her treasured amethyst brooch and now sat there calmly reciting the details thereof without the least apparent compunction or repentance.

"Anne, this is terrible," she said, trying to speak calmly. "You are the very wickedest girl I ever heard of."

"Yes, I suppose I am," agreed Anne tranquilly. "And I know I'll have to be punished. It'll be your duty to punish me, Marilla. Won't you please get it over right off because I'd like to go to the picnic with nothing on my mind."

"Picnic, indeed! You'll go to no picnic today, Anne Shirley! That shall be your punishment. And it isn't half severe enough either for what you've done!"

"Not go to the picnic!" Anne sprang to her feet and clutched Marilla's hand. "But you *promised* me I might! Oh, Marilla, I must go to the picnic. That was why I confessed. Punish me any way you like but that. Oh, Marilla, please, please, let me go to the picnic. Think of the ice cream! For anything you know I may never have a chance to taste ice cream again."

Marilla disengaged Anne's clinging hands stonily.

"You needn't plead, Anne. You are not going to the picnic and that's final. No, not a word."

Anne realized that Marilla was not to be moved. She clasped her hands together, gave a piercing shriek, and then flung herself

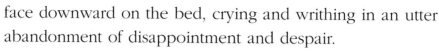

face downward on the bed, crying and writhing in an utter abandonment of disappointment and despair.

"For the land's sake!" gasped Marilla, hastening from the room. "I believe the child is crazy. No child in her senses would behave as she does. If she isn't she's utterly bad. Oh, dear, I'm afraid Rachel was right from the first. But I've put my hand to the plow, and I won't look back."

That was a dismal morning. Marilla worked fiercely and scrubbed the porch floor and the dairy shelves when she could find nothing else to do. Neither the shelves nor the porch needed it, but Marilla did. Then she went out and raked the yard.

When dinner was ready she went to the stairs and called Anne. A tear-stained face appeared, looking tragically over the banisters.

"Come down to your dinner, Anne."

"I don't want my dinner, Marilla," said Anne sobbingly. "I couldn't eat anything. My heart is broken. You'll feel remorse of conscience some day, I expect, for breaking it, Marilla, but I forgive you. Remember when the time comes that I forgive you. But please don't ask me to eat anything, especially boiled pork and greens. Boiled pork and greens are so unromantic when one is in affliction."

Exasperated, Marilla returned to the kitchen and poured out her tale of woe to Matthew, who, between his sense of justice and his unlawful sympathy with Anne, was a miserable man.

"Well now, she shouldn't have taken the brooch, Marilla, or told stories about it," he admitted, mournfully surveying his plateful of unromantic pork and greens as if he, like Anne, thought it a food unsuited to crises of feeling, "but she's such a little thing—such an interesting little thing. Don't you think it's pretty rough not to let her go to the picnic when she's so set on it?"

"Matthew Cuthbert, I'm amazed at you. I think I've let her off entirely too easy. And she doesn't appear to realize how wicked she's been at all—that's what worries me most. If she'd really felt sorry it wouldn't be so bad. And you don't seem to realize it neither; you're making excuses for her all the time to yourself— I can see that."

"Well now, she's such a little thing," feebly reiterated Matthew. "And there should be allowances made, Marilla. You know she's never had any bringing up."

"Well, she's having it now," retorted Marilla.

The retort silenced Matthew if it did not convince him. That dinner was a very dismal meal. The only cheerful thing about it was Jerry Buote, the hired boy, and Marilla resented his cheerfulness as a personal insult.

When her dishes were washed and her bread sponge set and her hens fed Marilla remembered that she had noticed a small rent in her best black lace shawl when she had taken it off on Monday afternoon on returning from the Ladies' Aid. She would go and mend it.

The shawl was in a box in her trunk. As Marilla lifted it out, the sunlight, falling through the vines that clustered thickly about the window, struck upon something caught in the shawl—something that glittered and sparkled in facets of violet light. Marilla snatched at it with a gasp. It was the amethyst brooch, hanging to a thread of the lace by its catch!

"Dear life and heart," said Marilla blankly, "what does this mean? Here's my brooch safe and sound that I thought was at the bottom of Barry's pond. Whatever did that girl mean by saying she took it and lost it? I declare I believe Green Gables is bewitched. I remember now that when I took off my shawl Monday afternoon I laid it on the bureau for a minute. I suppose the brooch got caught in it somehow. Well!"

Marilla betook herself to the east gable, brooch in hand. Anne had cried herself out and was sitting dejectedly by the window.

"Anne Shirley," said Marilla solemnly, "I've just found my brooch hanging to my black lace shawl. Now I want to know what that rigmarole you told me this morning meant."

"Why, you said you'd keep me here until I confessed," returned Anne wearily, "and so I decided to confess because I was bound to get to the picnic. I thought out a confession last night after I went to bed and made it as interesting as I could. And I said it over and over so that I wouldn't forget it. But you wouldn't let me go to the picnic after all, so all my trouble was wasted."

Marilla had to laugh in spite of herself. But her conscience pricked her.

"Anne, you do beat all! But I was wrong—I see that now. I shouldn't have doubted your word when I'd never known you to tell a story. Of course, it wasn't right for you to confess to a thing you hadn't done—it was very wrong to do so. But I drove you to it so if you'll forgive me, Anne, I'll forgive you and we'll start square again. And now get yourself ready for the picnic."

Anne flew up like a rocket.

"Oh, Marilla, isn't it too late?"

"No, it's only two o'clock. They won't be more than well gathered yet and it'll be an hour before they have tea. Wash your face and comb your hair and put on your gingham. I'll fill a basket for you. There's plenty of stuff baked in the house. And I'll get Jerry to hitch up the sorrel and drive you down to the picnic ground."

"Oh, Marilla," exclaimed Anne, flying to the washstand. "Five minutes ago I was so miserable I was wishing I'd never been born and now I wouldn't change places with an angel!"

That night a thoroughly happy, completely tired-out Anne

returned to Green Gables in a state of beatification impossible to describe.

"Oh, Marilla, I've had a perfectly scrumptious time. Scrumptious is a new word I learned today. I heard Mary Alice Bell use it. Isn't it very expressive? Everything was lovely. We had a splendid tea and then Mr. Harmon Andrews took us all for a row on the Lake of Shining Waters—six of us at a time. And Jane Andrews nearly fell overboard. She was leaning out to pick water lilies and if Mr. Andrews hadn't caught her by her sash just in the nick of time she'd have fallen in and prob'ly been drowned. I wish it had been me. It would have been such a romantic experience to have nearly drowned. It would be such a thrilling tale to tell. And we had the ice cream. Words fail me to describe that ice cream. Marilla, I assure you it was sublime."

That evening Marilla told the whole story to Matthew over her stocking basket.

"I'm willing to own up that I made a mistake," she concluded candidly, "but I've learned a lesson. I have to laugh when I think of Anne's 'confession,' although I suppose I shouldn't, for it really was a falsehood. But it doesn't seem as bad as the other would have been, somehow, and anyhow I'm responsible for it. That child is hard to understand in some respects. But I believe she'll turn out all right yet. And there's one thing certain, no house will ever be dull that she's in."

Introduction

Eleven-year-old Gilly is tough and resourceful. She has to be, to deal with the succession of foster families her social worker, Miss Ellis, places her with. Always at the back of Gilly's mind is the forlorn hope that her mother will come back for her. In the meantime, she uses her ingenuity and quick thinking as she moves from home to home: "I am too clever and too hard to manage. Gruesome Gilly, they call me." Will things be any different in the Trotter household, with Maime and her foster son William Ernest? It is only when Miss Ellis arrives to take her away after a particularly hairy incident, that Gilly realizes that perhaps Maime Trotter is on her side after all.

THE GREAT GILLY HOPKINS

KATHERINE PATERSON

Pow

There was a fight between Trotter and Miss Ellis. Gilly heard the sounds of battle in the living room when she came in from school the next afternoon. "Never, never, never!" Trotter was bellowing, like an old cow deprived of its calf.

Gilly stopped still in the hallway, closing the door without a sound.

"Mrs. Trotter, nobody at the agency looks at it as any indication of failure on your part—"

"You think I care what the agency thinks?"

"You're one of our most capable foster parents. You've been with us for more than twenty years. This won't affect your record with us. You're too valuable—"

"I don't give a spit about no record. You ain't taking Gilly."

"We're trying to think of you—"

"No, you ain't. If you was thinking of me, you'd never come to me with such a fool notion."

"This is a troubled child, Maime. She needs special—"

"No! I ain't giving her up. Never!"

"If you won't think of yourself, think of William Ernest. He's come too far in the last year to let—I've seen myself how she upsets him."

"It was William Ernest got her to come home last night." Trotter's voice was square and stubborn.

"Because he saw how upset you were. That doesn't mean she can't damage him."

"William Ernest has lived with me for over two years. He's gonna make it. I know he is. Sometimes, Miz Ellis, you gotta walk on your heel and favor your toe even if it makes your heel a little sore."

"I don't understand what you're driving at."

"Somebody's got to favor Gilly for a little while. She's long overdue."

"That's exactly it, Mrs. Trotter. I'm quite aware of Gilly's needs. I've been her caseworker for nearly five years, and whether you believe it or not, I really care about her. But I don't think it's her needs we're talking about right now, is it?"

"What do you mean?"

"It's *your* needs." Said very quietly.

A silence and then, "Yes, Lord knows, I need her." A funny broken sound like a sob came from Trotter. "I like to die when I found her gone."

"You can't do that, Mrs. Trotter. You can't let them tear you to pieces."

"Don't try to tell a mother how to feel."

"You're a foster mother, Mrs. Trotter." Miss Ellis's voice was firm. "You can't afford to forget that."

Gilly's whole body was engulfed in a great aching. She opened and slammed the front door, pretending to have just come in. This time they heard her.

"That you Gilly, honey?"

She went to the doorway of the living room. Both women were on their feet, flushed as though they'd been running a race.

"Well, Gilly," Miss Ellis began, voice glittering like a fake Christmas tree.

"Miz Ellis," Trotter broke in loudly, "was just saying how it's up to you." There was a flash of alarm from the social worker that Trotter pretended not to see. "You want to stay on here with William Ernest and me—that's fine. You want her to find you someplace else—that's fine, too. You got to be the one to decide." Her eyes shifted uneasily toward Miss Ellis.

"What about," Gilly asked, her mouth going dry as a stale soda cracker, "what about my real mother?"

Miss Ellis's eyebrows jumped. "I wrote her, Gilly, several months ago, when we decided to move you from the Nevinses. She never answered."

"She wrote me. She wants me to come out there."

Miss Ellis looked at Trotter. "Yes. I know about the postcard," the caseworker said.

Those damned cops reading people's mail and blabbing, passing it around, snickering over it probably.

"Gilly. If—if she had really wanted you with her—"

"She does want me. She said so!"

"Then why hasn't she come to get you?" A hard edge had come into Miss Ellis's voice, and her eyebrows were twitching madly.

"It's been over eight years, Gilly. Even when she lived close by, she never came to see you."

"It's different now!"—wasn't it?—"She's gonna come! She really wants me!"—didn't she?

Trotter came over to her and laid her arm heavily on Gilly's shoulder. "If she knowed you—if she just knowed what a girl she has—she'd be here in a minute."

Oh, Trotter, don't be a fool. If she knew what I was like, she'd never come. It takes someone stupid like you—Gilly removed herself gently from under the weighty embrace and addressed herself to Miss Ellis, eye to eyebrow.

"Till she comes . . . till she comes for me, I guess I'll just stay here."

Trotter wiped her face with her big hand and snuffled. "Well, I'm sure we'll be seeing you sometime, Miz Ellis."

The social worker wasn't going to be swept out quite so easily. She set her feet apart as though fearing Trotter might try to remove her bodily and said, "Officer Rhine told me when he called that you had well over a hundred dollars with you last night."

"Yeah?"

It came out sassy, but Miss Ellis just squinted her eyes and went on: "It's hard to believe that it was all your money."

"So?"

"So I call taking other people's money *stealing*, Miss Hopkins."

"Yeah?"

Trotter patted Gilly's arm as if to shush her. "So do we, Miz Ellis. Surely you don't think this is the first time something like this has happened to me over the last twenty years?"

"No, I know it's not."

"Then how 'bout trusting me to handle it?"

Miss Ellis shook her head and smoothed her trouser suit down over her rump before she put on her coat. "I'll be in close touch," she said.

Trotter nearly shoved her out the front door. "We're going to do just fine. Don't worry your pretty little head about us, hear?"

"I get paid to worry, Mrs. Trotter."

Trotter smiled impatiently and closed the door quickly. When she turned back towards Gilly, her face was like Mount Rushmore stone.

Gilly blinked in surprise at the sudden and absolute change.

"I don't take lightly to stealing, you know."

Gilly nodded. No use pretending sassiness.

"I figure that money ain't all mine, right?"

"No."

"Well, where'd you get it?"

"I found it," said Gilly softly.

Trotter came over and with two hands lifted Gilly's face to look into her own. "Where did you get it, Gilly?"

"I found it behind some books next door."

Trotter dropped her hands in disbelief. "You stole from Mr. Randolph?"

"It was just lying there behind the books. He probably didn't even—"

"Gilly, you stole it. Don't put no fancy name on it. It was his, and you took it, right?"

"I guess so."

"How much?"

"Uh, for—thir—"

"Don't fool with me. How much?"

"Forty-four dollars," Gilly said miserably.

"Well, you gotta take it back."

"I can't." Trotter stood there, hand on hip, staring at her until

Gilly continued, "I gave five dollars to Agnes Stokes."

"You did, huh?"

Gilly nodded.

"Well"—a great sigh—"I'll lend you the five to pay Mr. Randolph back, and you can work it off."

Giving back Mr. Randolph's money was not as bad as it might have been. The old man apparently had no idea that there had been any money behind his books. Either he'd forgotten, or it had been put there by his wife, dead long before Trotter's Melvin. At any rate, when Gilly gave the forty-four dollars to him, Trotter looming behind her like a mighty army, he accepted her mumbled explanation without showing shock or undue curiosity, but with a strange little dignity.

"Thank you," he said, for once not doubling the phrase. He put the money in his pocket, rubbed his hands together briefly, and then put out his hand to be led to supper.

Gilly hesitated for a moment, waiting for the sermon that was bound to pour forth, if not from him, surely from Trotter. But neither spoke, so she took Mr. Randolph's hand, instead of his elbow as she usually did, as a kind of thank you.

Trotter had obviously never heard of either the minimum wage or the child labor laws. She posted the following sign in the kitchen:

Washing dishes and cleaning kitchen   10¢
Vacuuming downstairs   10¢
Cleaning both bathrooms including floors   10¢
Dusting   10¢
Helping William Ernest with schoolwork, one hour   25¢

Gilly began to spend a lot of time with W.E. She discovered several things. One was that the boy was not as dumb as he looked. If you held back and didn't press him, he could often figure out things for himself, but when you crowded him, he would choke right up, and if you laughed at him, he'd throw his hands up as if to protect his head from a blow. It finally occurred to Gilly that he really thought she would smack him every time he made a mistake.

Which was why, of course, Trotter tiptoed around the boy as though he would shatter at the least commotion, and why she was death on anyone she caught fooling around with him.

But it wasn't going to work. W.E. wasn't a fluted antique cup in Mrs. Nevins's china cupboard. He was a kid—a foster kid. And if he didn't toughen up, what would happen to him when there was no Trotter to look after him?

So Gilly asked him, "What do you do when somebody socks you?"

His squinty little eyes went wild behind the glasses.

"I'm not going to hit you. I was just wondering what you do."

He stuck his right index finger into his mouth and began to tug at the nail.

She took out the finger and studied his stubby-nailed hand for a minute. "Nothing wrong with this, I can see. Ever think of smacking them back?"

He shook his head, wide-eyed.

"You going to go through life letting people pick on you?"

He hung his head. The finger went back in.

"Look, William Ernest"—she bent over close to his ear and whispered hoarsely into it—"I'm going to teach you how to fight. No charge or anything. Then when some big punk comes up to you and tries to start something, you can just let them have it."

His finger dropped from his mouth as he stared at her, unbelieving.

"You hear how I fought six boys one day—all by myself?"

He nodded solemnly.

"Before I get through with you, you're going to do the same thing. *Pow! Pow! Pow! Pow! Pow! Pow!*" She landed six imaginary punches sending six imaginary bullies flying.

"*Pow*," he echoed softly, tentatively doubling up his fist and giving a feeble swing.

"First thing, when somebody yells at you, don't throw your hands up"—she imitated him—"and act like you think they're going to kill you."

"*Pow?*" He swung his little fist in a kind of question mark.

"Naw, not *first* thing. See, they may not be even meaning to hit you. First thing is, you take a deep breath—" She filled her diaphragm and waited while he tried to imitate her, his ribs poking through his shirt. "Then you yell like this: *Get the hell outa my way!*"

Before the sentence was out, Trotter was filling the doorway like the wrath of God Almighty.

"OK, OK," Gilly said. "Leave out the hell part. The main thing—"

"What are you kids doing? I thought I was paying you to help William Ernest with his reading?"

"Naw. This is on my own time. No charge."

Trotter looked dubiously at W.E. He was standing on tiptoe, fists clenched, eyes squeezed shut in his red face, sucking in a huge breath.

"*Get the hell out my way!*" He turned to Gilly, smiling. "Was that good, Gilly?"

"Better leave the hell part out in front of Trotter. But that was pretty good for a start. Really not bad."

"Gilly," said Trotter.

"Look, Trotter. He's got to learn to take care of himself, and I'm the best damn—the best teacher around."

Trotter just went on standing in the doorway as though she couldn't think what to do next, when the little guy marched over to her, put his fists up in front of her huge bosom, took in a breath, and said squeakily, "Get out my way."

Tears started in the woman's eyes. She threw her arms around W.E. and bear-hugged him.

"I was just practicing, Trotter. I didn't mean you."

"I know, William Ernest, honey," she said. "I know."

"He's got to learn to take care of himself in the world, Trotter."

The big woman wiped her face with her apron and sniffed.

"Don't I know that, baby?" She patted the boy and straightened up. "How 'bout you finishing this lesson outside? I don't b'lieve it's something I want to listen to."

"C'mon, Gilly." William Ernest slid around Trotter and started for the back door. "*Pow! Pow!*" they could hear him exploding softly down the hall.

"I'm not going to teach him to pick on people," Gilly said, "just how to take care of himself. He can't come hiding behind your skirt every time someone looks at him cross-eyed."

"I s'pose not."

"Even real mothers can't watch out for kids the rest of their lives, and you're just his foster mother."

"So they keep telling me."

Gilly hadn't meant to be cruel, but she needed to make Trotter understand. "If he knows how to read and how to stick up for himself, he'll be OK."

"You got it all figured out, ain't you, Gilly, honey?" She relaxed into a smile. "Well, I ain't stopping your boxing lessons. I just don't care to watch."

Boxing lessons? The woman was a throwback to another century. Gilly started to pass her at the door, but as she brushed by the big body, Trotter grabbed her and planted a wet kiss on her forehead. One hand went up automatically to wipe the spot, but a look at Trotter's face, and Gilly stopped her arm midway.

"Don't know what got into me," Trotter mumbled, trying to turn it into a joke. "I know you don't allow no kissing. Sometimes I just haul off and go crazy."

"At Sunday school, Miss Applegate calls it demon possession."

"Does she now? Demon possession, is it?" She began to laugh so hard, Gilly could feel the boards vibrating under her feet. "Demon possession—Mercy, girl, I'd have to catch me a jet to keep one step ahead of you. Well—you better get going before the devil grabs me one more time."

She waved her hand to land a mock spank on Gilly's bottom, but by the time it swept the air, Gilly's bottom, along with the rest of her, was well down the hall.

Of the four March girls, it is fifteen-year-old Jo who likes to act as the head of the family now that their father is away fighting in the Civil War. In his letters home, he calls his daughters "Little Women" because they help their mother around the house during these difficult war years. Meg, the eldest, is sweet and patient, but sometimes in a muddle. Beth is shy and gentle. Amy, the baby of the family, is just a little self-important, but means well. Jo, a real tomboy, always wants to be doing something interesting or going somewhere exciting. She loves to act and to dress up, often taking the male roles, like the time at Christmas when they put on a special play for their friends. After the show, they tuck into the most splendid feast, provided by their neighbor, old Mr. Laurence, and delivered by his grandson, "the Laurence boy." Jo would like to know the Laurence boy better. Perhaps there will be an opportunity in the not too distant future. . . .

LITTLE WOMEN

LOUISA MAY ALCOTT

The Laurence Boy

"Jo! Jo! Where are you?" cried Meg, at the foot of the garret stairs.

"Here!" answered a husky voice from above; and running up, Meg found her sister eating apples and crying over the *Heir of Redcliffe,* wrapped up in a comforter on an old three-legged sofa by the sunny window. This was Jo's favorite refuge; and here she loved to retire with half-a-dozen russets and a nice book, to enjoy the quiet and the society of a pet rat who lived nearby, and didn't mind her a particle. As Meg appeared, Scrabble whisked into his hole. Jo shook the tears off her cheeks, and waited to hear the news.

"Such fun! Only see! A regular note of invitation from Mrs. Gardiner for tomorrow night!" cried Meg, waving the precious

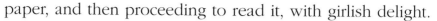

paper, and then proceeding to read it, with girlish delight.

"'Mrs. Gardiner would be happy to see Miss March and Miss Josephine at a little dance on New Year's Eve.' Marmee is willing we should go; now what *shall* we wear?"

"What's the use of asking that, when you know we shall wear our poplins, because we haven't got anything else?" answered Jo, with her mouth full.

"If I only had a silk!" sighed Meg. "Mother says I may when I'm eighteen, perhaps; but two years is an everlasting time to wait."

"I'm sure our pops look like silk, and they are nice enough for us. Yours is as good as new, but I forgot the burn and the tear in mine. Whatever shall I do? The burn shows badly, and I can't take any out."

"You must sit still all you can, and keep your back out of sight; the front is all right. I shall have a new ribbon in my hair, and Marmee will lend me her little pearl pin, and my new slippers are lovely, and my gloves will do, though they aren't as nice as I'd like."

"Mine are spoilt with lemonade, and I can't get any new ones, so I shall have to go without," said Jo, who never troubled herself much about dress.

"You *must* have gloves, or I won't go," cried Meg decidedly. "Gloves are more important than anything else; you can't dance without them, and if you don't I should be *so* mortified."

"Then I'll stay still. I don't care much for company dancing; it's no fun to go sailing around; I like to fly about and cut capers."

"You can't ask mother for new ones, they are so expensive, and you are so careless. She said, when you spoilt the others, that she shouldn't get you any more this winter. Can't you make them do?" asked Meg anxiously.

"I can hold them crumpled up in my hand, so no one will know how stained they are; that's all I can do. No! I'll tell you how we can manage—each wear one good one and carry a bad one; don't you see?"

"Your hands are bigger than mine, and you will stretch my glove dreadfully," began Meg, whose gloves were a tender point with her.

"Then I'll go without. I don't care what people say!" cried Jo, taking up her book.

"You may have it, you may! Only don't stain it, and do behave nicely. Don't put your hands behind you, or stare, or say 'Christopher Columbus!' will you?"

"Don't worry about me; I'll be as prim as I can, and not get into any scrapes, if I can help it. Now go and answer your note, and let me finish this splendid story."

So Meg went away to "accept with thanks," look over her dress, and sing blithely as she did up her one real lace frill; while Jo finished her story, her four apples, and had a game of romps with Scrabble.

On New Year's Eve, the parlor was deserted, for the two younger girls played dressing-maids, and the two elder were absorbed in the all-important business of "getting ready for the party." Simple as the toilets were, there was a great deal of running up and down, laughing and talking, and at one time a strong smell of burned hair pervaded the house. Meg wanted a few curls about her face, and Jo undertook to pinch the papered locks with a pair of hot tongs.

"Ought they to smoke like that?" asked Beth, from her perch on the bed.

"It's the dampness drying," replied Jo.

"What a queer smell! It's like burnt feathers," observed Amy, smoothing her own pretty curls with a superior air.

"There, now I'll take off the papers and you'll see a cloud of little ringlets," said Jo, putting down the tongs.

She did take off the papers, but no cloud of ringlets appeared, for the hair came with the papers, and the horrified hairdresser laid a row of little scorched bundles on the bureau before her victim.

"Oh, oh, oh! What *have* you done? I'm spoilt! I can't go! My hair, oh, my hair!" wailed Meg, looking with despair at the uneven frizzle on her forehead.

"Just my luck! You shouldn't have asked me to do it; I always spoil everything. I'm so sorry, but the tongs were too hot, and so I've made a mess," groaned poor Jo, regarding the black pancakes with tears of regret.

"It isn't spoilt; just frizzle it, and tie your ribbon so the ends come on your forehead a bit, and it will look like the last fashion. I've seen many girls do it so," said Amy consolingly.

"Serves me right for trying to be fine. I wish I'd let my hair alone," cried Meg petulantly.

"So do I, it was so smooth and pretty. But it will soon grow out again," said Beth, coming to kiss and comfort the shorn sheep.

After various lesser mishaps, Meg was finished at last, and by the united exertions of the family, Jo's hair was got up, and her dress on. They looked very well in their simple suits—Meg in silvery drab, with a blue velvet snood, lace frills, and the pearl pin; Jo in maroon, with a stiff, gentlemanly linen collar, and a white chrysanthemum or two for her only ornament. Each put on one nice light glove, and carried one soiled one, and all pronounced the effect "quite easy and fine," Meg's high-heeled slippers were very tight, and hurt her, though she would not own it, and Jo's nineteen hair pins all seemed stuck straight into her head, which was not exactly comfortable; but, dear me, let us be elegant or die!

"Have a good time, dearies," said Mrs. March, as the sisters went daintily down the walk. "Don't eat much supper, and come away at eleven, when I send Hannah for you." As the gate clashed behind them, a voice cried from a window—

"Girls, girls! *have* you both got nice pocket-handkerchiefs?"

"Yes, yes, spandy nice, and Meg has cologne on hers," cried Jo, adding, with a laugh, as they went on, "I do believe Marmee would ask that if we were all running away from an earthquake."

"It is one of her aristocratic tastes, and quite proper, for a real lady is always known by neat boots, gloves, and handkerchief," replied Meg, who had a good many little "aristocratic tastes" of her own.

"Now don't forget to keep the bad breadth out of sight, Jo. Is my sash right? And does my hair look *very* bad?" said Meg, as she turned from the glass in Mrs. Gardiner's dressing room, after a prolonged prink.

"I know I shall forget. If you see me doing anything wrong, just remind me by a wink, will you?" returned Jo, giving her collar a twitch, and her head a hasty brush.

"No, winking isn't ladylike; I'll lift my eyebrows if anything is wrong, and nod if you are all right. Now hold your shoulders straight, and take short steps, and don't shake hands if you are introduced to anyone, it isn't the thing."

"How *do* you learn all the proper ways? I never can. Isn't that music gay?"

Down they went, feeling a trifle timid, for they seldom went to parties, and, informal as this little gathering was, it was an event to them. Mrs. Gardiner, a stately old lady, greeted them kindly, and handed them over to the eldest of her six daughters. Meg knew Sallie, and was at her ease very soon; but Jo, who didn't care much for girls or girlish gossip, stood about with her back carefully against the wall, and felt as much out of place as a colt in a flower garden. Half-a-dozen jovial lads were talking about skates in another part of the room, and she longed to go and join them, for skating was one of the joys of her life. She telegraphed her wish to Meg, but the eyebrows went up so alarmingly that she dared not stir. No one came to talk to her, and one by one the group near her dwindled away, till she was left alone. She could not roam about and amuse herself for the burned breadth would show, so she stared at people rather forlornly till the dancing began. Meg was asked at once, and the tight slippers tripped about so briskly that none would have guessed the pain their wearer suffered smilingly. Jo saw a big, redheaded youth approaching her corner, and fearing he meant to engage her, she slipped into a curtained recess, intending to peep and enjoy herself in peace. Unfortunately, another bashful person had chosen the same refuge; for, as the curtain fell behind her, she found herself face to face with the "Laurence boy."

"Dear me, I didn't know anyone was here!" stammered Jo, preparing to back out as speedily as she had bounced in.

But the boy laughed, and said pleasantly, though he looked a little startled,—

"Don't mind me; stay if you like."

"Shan't I disturb you?"

"Not a bit; I only came here because I don't know many people, and felt rather strange at first, you know."

"So did I. Don't go away, please, unless you'd rather."

The boy sat down again and looked at his pumps, till Jo said, trying to be polite and easy,—

"I think I've had the pleasure of seeing you before; you live near us, don't you?"

"Next door;" and he looked up and laughed outright, for Jo's prim manner was rather funny when he remembered how they had chatted about cricket when he brought the cat home.

That put Jo at her ease; and she laughed too, as she said, in her heartiest way,—

"We did have such a good time over your nice Christmas present."

"Grandpa sent it."

"But you put it into his head, didn't you, now?"

"How is your cat, Miss March?" asked the boy, trying to look sober, while his black eyes shone with fun.

"Nicely, thank you, Mr. Laurence; but I am not Miss March, I'm only Jo," returned the young lady.

"I'm not Mr. Laurence; I'm only Laurie."

"Laurie Laurence—what an odd name."

"My first name is Theodore, but I don't like it, for the fellows called me Dora, so I made them say Laurie instead."

"I hate my name, too—so sentimental! I wish every one would say Jo, instead of Josephine. How did you make the boys stop calling you Dora?"

"I thrashed 'em."

"I can't thrash Aunt March, so I suppose I shall have to bear it;" and Jo resigned herself with a sigh.

"Don't you like to dance, Miss Jo?" asked Laurie, as if he thought the name suited her.

"I like it well enough if there is plenty of room, and everyone is lively. In a place like this, I'm sure to upset something, tread on people's toes, or do something dreadful, so I keep out of mischief, and let Meg sail about. Don't you dance?"

"Sometimes; you see I've been abroad a good many years, and haven't been into company enough yet to know how you do things here."

"Abroad!" cried Jo. "Oh, tell me about it! I love to hear people describe their travels."

Laurie didn't seem to know where to begin; but Jo's eager

questions soon set him going, and he told her how he had been at school in Vevey, where the boys never wore hats, and had a fleet of boats on the lake, and for holiday fun went on walking trips about Switzerland with their teachers.

"Don't I wish I'd been there!" cried Jo. "Did you go to Paris?"

"We spent last winter there."

"Can you talk French?"

"We were not allowed to speak anything else at Vevey."

"Do say some. I can read it, but can't pronounce."

"*Quel nom a cette jeune demoiselle en les pantoufles jolis?*" said Laurie good-naturedly.

"How nicely you do it! Let me see—you said, 'Who is the young lady in the pretty slippers?', didn't you?"

"*Oui, mademoiselle.*"

"It's my sister Margaret, and you knew it was! Do you think she is pretty?"

"Yes; she makes me think of the German girls, she looks so fresh and quiet, and dances like a lady."

Jo quite glowed with pleasure at this boyish praise of her sister, and stored it up to repeat to Meg. Both peeped and criticized and chatted, till they felt like old acquaintances. Laurie's bashfulness soon wore off, for Jo's gentlemanly demeanor amused and set him at his ease, and Jo was her merry self again, because her dress was forgotten, and nobody lifted their eyebrows at her. She liked the "Laurence boy" better than ever, and took several good looks at him, so that she might describe him to the girls; for they had no brothers, very few male cousins, and boys were almost unknown creatures to them.

"Curly black hair, brown skin, big black eyes, handsome nose, fine teeth, small hands and feet, taller than I am; very polite for a boy, and altogether jolly. Wonder how old he is?"

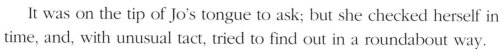

It was on the tip of Jo's tongue to ask; but she checked herself in time, and, with unusual tact, tried to find out in a roundabout way.

"I suppose you are going to college soon? I see you pegging away at your books—no, I mean studying hard," and Jo blushed at the dreadful "pegging" which had escaped her.

Laurie smiled, but didn't seem shocked, and answered with a shrug,—

"Not for a year or two; I won't go before seventeen, anyway."

"Aren't you but fifteen?" asked Jo, looking at the tall lad whom she had imagined seventeen already.

"Sixteen next month."

"How I wish I was going to college! You don't look as if you liked it."

"I hate it! Nothing but grinding or skylarking. And I don't like the way fellows do either, in this country."

"What do you like?"

"To live in Italy, and to enjoy myself in my own way."

Jo wanted very much to ask what his own way was; but his black brows looked rather threatening as he knit them, so she changed the subject by saying, as her foot kept time, "That's a splendid polka! Why don't you go and try it?"

"If you come too," he answered, with a gallant little bow.

"I can't; for I told Meg I wouldn't, because"—There Jo stopped, and looked undecided whether to tell or to laugh.

"Because what?" asked Laurie curiously.

"You won't tell?"

"Never!"

"Well, I have a bad trick of standing before the fire, and so burn my frocks, and I scorched this one; and, though it's nicely mended, it shows, and Meg told me to keep still, so no one would see it. You may laugh if you want to; it is funny, I know."

But Laurie didn't laugh; he only looked down a minute, and the expression of his face puzzled Jo, when he said very gently,—

"Never mind that; I'll tell you how we can manage: there's a long hall out there, and we can dance grandly, and no one will see us. Please come?"

Jo thanked him, and gladly went, wishing she had two neat gloves, when she saw the nice pearl-colored ones her partner wore. The hall was empty, and they had a grand polka, for Laurie danced well, and taught her the German step, which delighted Jo, being full of swing and spring.

Louisa May Alcott (1832–88) was born in Pennsylvania. She worked as a teacher, seamstress, and domestic servant, and as an army nurse during the Civil War. She also edited a children's magazine. Her most famous novel, *Little Women*, was published in two parts in 1868 and 1869, and is regarded as the first family story written for children. The character of Jo is based largely on Louisa May Alcott herself, and the author's sisters served as models for the other March girls.

L(yman) Frank Baum (1856–1919) was born in Chittenago, New York. During his varied career he worked as a newspaper reporter, a poultry farmer, a comic actor, and a traveling salesman (of Baum's Ever-Ready Castorine axle grease). He was also a founding director of the Oz Film Manufacturing Company in Los Angeles. He wrote nearly one hundred books (some published under pseudonyms), but it is for the enduringly popular *The Wonderful Wizard of Oz* (published in 1900) that he is best remembered. It was followed by over twenty more books about the land of Oz—which got its name from the letters O–Z on his filing cabinet drawer!

Joyce Lankester Brisley (1896–1978) was born in Sussex, England. She began writing and illustrating at an early age, and had her first story published in a children's magazine when she was thirteen. She studied at Lambeth Art School for two years and at the age of twenty had some of her pictures exhibited at the Royal Academy in London. Her most famous character, Milly-Molly-Mandy, first appeared in *The Christian Science Monitor* in 1925, and she went on to write and illustrate many popular stories about the little girl in the pink and white striped dress.

Frances Hodgson Burnett (1849–1924) was born in Manchester, England, but emigrated with her mother to Tennessee at the age of sixteen. Her first stories were published three years later and she became a prolific writer for both adults and children. Sara Crewe first appeared in a story in 1888, which became a play in 1902, and finally a full-length novel, *A Little Princess*, in 1905. It is for this book, together with two of her other children's novels, *Little Lord Fauntleroy* (1886) and *The Secret Garden* (1911), that she is best remembered.

Lewis Carroll (1832–98) was the pseudonym of Charles Lutwidge Dodgson, who was born in Cheshire, England. He was the eldest in a family of eleven, and as a child, he edited his own magazines. *Alice's Adventures in Wonderland* began as a story to entertain Alice Liddell, one of the daughters of the Dean of Oxford University's Christ Church College, where Charles Dodgson was a lecturer in mathematics. The book was published in 1865 and was followed in 1871 by *Through the Looking Glass, and What Alice Found There*.

Beverly Cleary was born in 1916 in Oregon. Of her many successful books, those featuring the exploits of Ramona Quimby, her sister Beezus, their friend Henry, and his dog Ribsy are probably the most popular. Ramona herself first appeared in 1950 in *Henry Huggins,* and there are now over a dozen titles in the series. *Ramona the Pest* was published in 1968. Beverly Cleary has received many awards for her writing, including the American Library Association's Laura Ingalls Wilder Award (for *Ramona the Brave* in 1975) and the Newbery Medal (for *Ramona Forever* in 1984).

Susan Coolidge (1835–1905) was the pseudonym of Sarah Chauncy Woolsey, who was born in Ohio. During the Civil War she worked in hospitals and helped organize a national nursing service. Later she became a literary critic and worked as a consultant for a Boston publisher. She is best known for creating the character of Katy Carr, the feisty heroine of *What Katy Did*, published in 1872 and the first of five Katy novels.

Roald Dahl (1916–90) was born in Wales to Norwegian parents. He was an R.A.F. fighter pilot during World War II, and it was while he was stationed in Washington as Assistant Air Attaché that he began to write the short stories that he is so well known for. His novels include *James and the Giant Peach* (1961), *Charlie and the Chocolate Factory* (1964), and *The BFG* (1982). Many of his novels, such as *The Witches* (1983 winner of the Whitbread Children's Novel Award) and *Matilda* (1988 winner of the Children's Book Award), have been made into popular movies. Quentin Blake's gloriously distinctive illustrations have become synonymous with Roald Dahl's books for children.

Astrid Lindgren was born in 1907 in Vimmerby, Sweden. She began her writing career by winning a children's book competition in 1944 and later became a children's book editor. She has published over forty novels and received numerous accolades, including the International Hans Christian Andersen Award and the International Book Award. Her most famous character, the irrepressible Pippi Longstocking, first appeared in 1950, and the series of books about her continues to be hugely popular around the world.

L(ucy) M(aud) Montgomery (1874–1942) was born on Prince Edward Island, Canada. She became a schoolteacher and later a postmistress, and worked as a journalist as well as a novelist. She was the author of many novels, most notably *Anne of Green Gables*, published in 1908 and the first of six books about the lively red-haired heroine. These were followed by other books such as *Rainbow Valley* and *Rilla of Ingleside* in which Anne also appears. Other popular L. M. Montgomery heroines include Emily Byrd Starr, whose trilogy began with *Emily of New Moon*, published in 1923.

Jill Murphy was born in 1949 in London, England. She has been writing stories since she was four years old, and drawing for as long as she can remember. She is the creator of many popular picture books, including *Five Minutes' Peace* (winner of the Best Books for Babies Award) and *The Last Noo-Noo* (winner of the Smarties Prize). Her series of novels about Mildred Hubble began in 1974 with the publication of *The Worst Witch*. There are now four titles in the series, all illustrated by the author.

Katherine Paterson was born in 1932 in China, where she lived until the age of eight when her family returned to the United States. She has worked as both a missionary and a teacher and is the author of many books for children. She has received several major awards for her writing, including the American Library Association's Newbery Medal in 1978 for *Bridge to Terabithia* and in 1981 for *Jacob Have I Loved*. *The Great Gilly Hopkins* was published in 1978. In 1988, she received the Regina Medal for her contribution to children's literature.

Eleanor H(odgman) Porter (1868–1920) was born in New Hampshire. A choir and concert singer, she trained at the prestigious New England Conservatory of Music in Boston. She wrote many books and became an overnight success with *Pollyanna*, published in 1913. Along with its sequel, *Pollyanna Grows Up*, it has remained popular ever since. In fact, Pollyanna's success was such that after the author's death, other writers were commissioned to continue her story. In all, a further ten Pollyanna books by four other writers were published.

Johanna Spyri (1827–1901) was born in Switzerland, in a village overlooking Lake Zurich, with glorious views of the Alps. Her father was a local doctor. Although very little is known about her life, she became the author of almost fifty novels. *Heidi* (whose original German title is *Heidi's Years of Wandering and Learning*) was published in 1880. It was soon translated into English and quickly became, and remains, her most popular book.

Ethel Turner (1870–1958) was born in Yorkshire, England, and emigrated to Australia at the age of ten. She was a children's book editor and magazine columnist and editor, as well as the author of over forty books. Her classic novel *Seven Little Australians* was published in 1894 and was the first realistic Australian family story. Ethel Turner went on to write three more books—*The Family At Misrule*, *Little Mother Meg*, and *Judy and Punch*—that follow the lives of the Woolcot family as they grow up.

Laura Ingalls Wilder (1867–1957) was born in Wisconsin. Her pioneer family lived an isolated life of self-sufficiency in a log cabin built by Laura's father, and they were always ready to move on in their covered wagon. Laura became a schoolteacher and did not begin writing down her vivid childhood memories until she was in her sixties. *Little House in the Big Woods* was published in 1932, the first in a series of nine absorbing books about her life.

ACKNOWLEDGMENTS

The publisher would like to thank the copyright holders for permission to reproduce the following copyright material:

Quentin Blake: A.P. Watt Ltd. for illustrations by Quentin Blake from *Matilda* by Roald Dahl, from *The Roald Dahl Treasury*, Jonathan Cape Ltd. 1997. Copyright © Quentin Blake 1997. **Joyce Lankester Brisley**: Kingfisher Publications Plc for text and illustrations from "Milly-Molly-Mandy Gives a Party" from *Milly-Molly-Mandy Stories* by Joyce Lankester Brisley, George G. Harrap & Co. Ltd. 1928. Copyright © 1928 Joyce Lankester Brisley. **Beverly Cleary**: Morrow Junior Books, a division of William Morrow & Co. Inc., for "The Baddest Witch in the World" from *Ramona the Pest* by Beverly Cleary, Avon Books 1968. Copyright © 1968 Beverly Cleary. **Roald Dahl**: David Higham Associates for "Arithmetic" from *Matilda* by Roald Dahl, Jonathan Cape Ltd. 1988. Copyright © 1988 Roald Dahl. **Laura Ingalls Wilder**: HarperCollins Publishers, Inc. for "Christmas" from *Little House in the Big Woods* by Laura Ingalls Wilder, Harper 1932. Copyright © 1932 Laura Ingalls Wilder. Copyright renewed © 1959 Roger Lea MacBride. "Little House" ® is a registered trademark of HarperCollins Publishers, Inc. **Astrid Lindgren**: Kerstin Kvint Literary & Co-Production Agency for "Pippi Goes to the Circus" from *Pippi Longstocking* by Astrid Lindgren, Rabén & Sjogren 1945. Copyright © Astrid Lindgren 1945. Viking Penguin, a division of Penguin Putnam, Inc. for translation by Florence Lamborn, copyright © 1950 Viking Press, Inc. Copyright renewed © 1978 Viking Penguin Inc. **L.M. Montgomery**: David Macdonald, trustee, and Ruth Macdonald, heirs of L.M. Montgomery for "Anne's Confession" from *Anne of Green Gables* by L.M. Montgomery, Boston and Toronto, Page, and London, Pitman 1908. Entered at Stationer's Hall. Copyright © 1984 David Macdonald, trustee, and Ruth Macdonald. "Anne of Green Gables" is a trademark of the Anne of Green Gables Licensing Authority Inc., used under license by Kingfisher Publications Plc "L.M. Montgomery" is a trademark of the Heirs of L.M. Montgomery Inc. **Jill Murphy:** A.P. Watt Ltd. for Chapter 4 and illustrations from *The Worst Witch* by Jill Murphy, Puffin 1978. Copyright © Jill Murphy 1974. Penguin Books U.K. Ltd. for title page illustration by Jill Murphy from *The Puffin Treasury of Children's Stories*. Puffin Books 1996. Copyright © Jill Murphy 1974, 1996. **Katherine Paterson:** HarperCollins Publishers, Inc. for "Pow" from *The Great Gilly Hopkins* by Katherine Paterson, Crowell 1978. Copyright © Katherine Paterson 1978. **Johanna Spyri**: "A Day With the Goats" from *Heidi* by Johanna Spyri, translated by Eileen Hall, Puffin 1956. **Sir John Tenniel**: Macmillan Children's Books for original illustrations by Sir John Tenniel colored by Harry Theaker and Diz Wallis from *Alice's Adventures in Wonderland* by Lewis Carroll, Macmillan Children's Books 1995. Illustrations colored by Harry Theaker, copyright © 1911 Macmillan Publishers Ltd. Illustrations colored by Diz Wallis, copyright © 1995 Macmillan Publishers Ltd. **Ethel Turner**: Penguin Books Australia Ltd. for "The General Sees Active Service" from *Seven Little Australians* by Ethel Turner, Puffin 1994. First published by Ward Lock 1894. Copyright © 1988 Philippa Poole.

Every effort has been made to obtain permission to reproduce copyright material, but there may be cases where we have been unable to trace a copyright holder. The publisher will be happy to correct any omissions in future printings.

The publisher would like to thank the following artists for their original illustrations:

Ian Beck: illustrations for *The Wizard of Oz* copyright © Ian Beck 1999. **Mick Brownfield**: illustrations for *The Great Gilly Hopkins* copyright © Mick Brownfield 1999. **Emma Chichester Clark**: illustrations for *A Little Princess* copyright © Emma Chichester Clark 1999. **Kady MacDonald Denton**: illustrations for *Little House in the Big Woods* copyright © Kady MacDonald Denton 1999. **Mark Edwards**: illustrations for *Anne of Green Gables* copyright © Mark Edwards 1999. **Anne Yvonne Gilbert**: illustrations for *Little Women* copyright © Anne Yvonne Gilbert 1999. **Felicity Gill**: illustrations for *Heidi* copyright © Felicity Gill 1999. **Rob Hefferan**: illustrations for *Seven Little Australians* copyright © Rob Hefferan 1999. **Alison Jay**: illustrations for *What Katy Did* copyright © Alison Jay 1999. **Susie Jenkin-Pearce**: illustrations for *Pollyanna* copyright © Susie Jenkin-Pearce 1999. **Chris Riddell**: illustrations for *Pippi Longstocking* copyright © Chris Riddell 1999. **Tony Ross**: illustrations for *Ramona the Pest* copyright © Tony Ross 1999.